MURDER MIDAIR

MURDER MIDAIR

TAKING OFF IS JUST THE BEGINNING—LANDING COULD BE THE END . . . OF YOUR LIFE!

JAMES AUSTIN

iUniverse, Inc.
Bloomington

Murder Midair
Taking Off Is Just the Beginning—Landing Could Be the End . . .
of Your Life!

Copyright © 2013 by James Austin.

All rights reserved. No part of this book may be used or reproduced by any means, graphic, electronic, or mechanical, including photocopying, recording, taping or by any information storage retrieval system without the written permission of the publisher except in the case of brief quotations embodied in critical articles and reviews.

This is a work of fiction. All of the characters, names, incidents, organizations, and dialogue in this novel are either the products of the author's imagination or are used fictitiously.

iUniverse books may be ordered through booksellers or by contacting:

iUniverse
1663 Liberty Drive
Bloomington, IN 47403
www.iuniverse.com
1-800-Authors (1-800-288-4677)

Because of the dynamic nature of the Internet, any web addresses or links contained in this book may have changed since publication and may no longer be valid. The views expressed in this work are solely those of the author and do not necessarily reflect the views of the publisher, and the publisher hereby disclaims any responsibility for them.

Any people depicted in stock imagery provided by Thinkstock are models, and such images are being used for illustrative purposes only.
Certain stock imagery © Thinkstock.

ISBN: 978-1-4759-6447-9 (sc)
ISBN: 978-1-4759-6449-3 (hc)
ISBN: 978-1-4759-6448-6 (ebk)

Library of Congress Control Number: 2012923074

Printed in the United States of America

iUniverse rev. date: 01/30/2013

For Arthur

Nos coeurs ont maintenant communiqué
Jour après jour l'amour nous attache
Maintenant et pour toujours
Nous sommes l'amour
Par vos yeux je vois l'amour
Par votre coeur je sens l'amour
Dans nos âmes
Nous sommes aimés
James Austin

I dedicate this book to Arthur Stempert.
My teacher
My friend
My love
C.JA.J.

ACKNOWLEDGEMENTS

I would like to thank Jenny Styles for all her advise, input and encouragment throughout this project and for putting up with the constant rambling's. Your help was paramount to me.

To Anthony Sarks and the staff of Ricardoes Tomatoes in Port Macquarie for all the encouragement.

To my sister Deirdre, father Des and the rest of my family and friends for the encouragement and well wishes.

To all at iUniverse who helped in making the goal acheivable and for all the advise and knowledge you passed on to me.

To those who find enjoyment from my work, I thank you.

James

CONTENTS

(1) Wynonna 1
(2) The Producer's Assistant 5
(3) Jennifer and Orla 8
(4) Two-gether Forever 11
(5) Preparing to Fly 14
(6) Stormy Weather 17
(7) Please Be Seated 20
(8) Mystery Man 24
(9) The In-Flight Entertainment 28
(10) Thelma and Millicent 32
(11) The Crew 35
(12) Drinks, Anyone? 39
(13) Reunited . . . and It Feels so Good! 43
(14) At Your Service 46
(15) Join the Club 48
(16) How a Conversation Ended Up in the Toilet ... 52
(17) Business as Not-So-Usual 56
(18) A Meeting of Two Minds 60
(19) Attention All Passengers 64
(20) Come and Get It! 68
(21) Wynonna Has Spoken! 73
(22) The Cleanup 76
(23) Trick or Treat 80
(24) The Descent 84
(25) Death of a Diva 87

(26) Hide the Donuts—It's the Fuzz 90
(27) Exit, Stage Right! 93
(28) It's Question Time 96
(29) The Investigation 99
(30) Cold Case 103

(1)

WYNONNA

"Oh no, no no, my dear, you don't belong on Broadway. I see you flying high, honey. Spread your wings and take flight. The sky is the limit."

"Are you saying I should go to Hollywood? You think I should do movies instead? Television? Do you see me making it as a huge star, Miss Bertrand?"

"Oh, sweetheart, no, silly girl, I see you as an air hostess. Now fuck off!"

Wynonna Bertrand: actress of stage and screen and lover to anyone who breathed in her vicinity. A self-made woman who took control of everything she did and everyone she knew. A bitch to all who had graced the stage with her. She was well-known around the entertainment elite as someone to not cross in business and in bed. It was her way or get out, end of story.

She was born on the worn side of town and to the wrong people—her own words. She never saw her parents as such; they were merely people to give her shelter until she was able to drift on her own terms. Wynonna decided fourteen was the right age and she never looked back. Wynonna knew how to get things done her way and would do anything to do just that. She had also been hiding a very, very dark secret.

Wynonna had a knack for getting the right parts and knocking anyone who got in her way right off the page. Now she was fifty-three and hating it. Her auburn hair needed coloring more often and she needed contacts to make her green eyes see the scripts more clearly, but her temper had not faded one bit. Wynonna did not like the fact that she was once the darling of Hollywood and she couldn't stand all these new-star sluts pushing their way onto her turf. Publicity tramps, the lot of them, getting not only their faces in the tabloids, but now they seemed to like showing the rest of themselves as well.

"They don't have one ounce of decency! Who gets out of a car not wearing underwear, knowing the paparazzi are all around, spreading their legs for the entire world to see they ain't no virgins?"

Truth be told, Wynonna once asked her publicity agent if she should do a similar thing, but that idea was locked away and the key destroyed.

"Playing a mother to one of these child whores will never happen," she had said on numerous occasions.

It was well-known in Hollywood that by absolutely no means did one ever offer Wynonna Bertrand an old-woman role—and that was one reason why the offers were becoming less and less. She was now on her way to audition for a movie being directed by her one-time lover, Bruce McFeeney, in LA. Wynonna was pissed she had to not only audition for the part—she thought she should be automatically cast in the role—but also because she had to travel on a commercial flight to do so. Wynonna was aware she was fast being pushed aside by new and more attractive options in the eyes of the studio executives, in the form of younger actresses who, just like the famous Wynonna Bertrand, would stop at nothing to land a role.

The part she was going to audition for was for a female CEO with a terminal illness who had to make a decision on who would be taking over when she passed. The character was also in her early forties, something the studio heads had a hard time being convinced of when they heard Wynonna was being considered for the part. She knew exactly what to do to get the part—or more to the point, *who* to do. It was a part that most fifty-three-year-old actors would not dare try. She had already made up her mind and nobody stood a chance.

Wynonna's flight was leaving JFK at 10:30 a.m. and the limousine was arranged to pick her up at the Plaza Hotel at 8:00

a.m. It was now 9:00 p.m. the night before and Wynonna had just sat down to dinner with a man whom she referred to as one of her East Coast lovers: Michael Dunn, a New York theater actor who liked to play around and not just on stage. Michael was a fan of bedding as many cast members as possible, male and female and at times all at once. Orgies were his thing. At twenty-five, he didn't have much trouble convincing anyone to join him in the sack. His shoulder-length blond hair, blue eyes and killer body were his draw cards. He had known Wynonna for about four years, ever since she saw him on stage during his Broadway debut. He didn't make it to the cast party that night but instead partied with Wynonna. Since then he had become the private property of Ms. Wynonna Bertrand—at least, that was what she thought. *What the old crow doesn't know can't hurt me*, he thought.

"Michael, darling, how are you, sweetness? How was rehearsal? I need you now!"

"Hi, Wynonna. I'm great, rehearsal was fine and can we eat first? I'm starved. Oh and I have a new move I want to try on you. One of the guys was telling me about it today. If all goes well, I think you'll scream the walls down. But first let me see a menu."

He was referring to a conversation he'd had in the dressing room during the day's rehearsals. One of the cast, Todd Perkins, told him about his escapades the previous night with a fan who would allow anything, just to be with an actor. He told Michael about his new technique, which involved using an adjustable clamp and an ice cube. "They will be on the ceiling," he added.

"What the fuck do you do with that?" Michael demanded, thinking more and more that this guy was filth on toast.

Todd told him, "Use some imagination." Then he added, "The ice cube, if used properly, will send them into orbit." He then left with a huge smile on his face.

That boy is sick, Michael thought as he wrote down "adjustable clamp at hardware store" on some paper and placed it in his pocket.

"You cad. You can eat all you want here, but you must eat my dessert upstairs," Wynonna informed him after hearing his story.

"Ooo, why, Miss Bertrand, I never. What type of a boy do you think I am?"

"My dear, you know and everyone else in this god-forsaken town knows what type of boy you are. Blind fucking Freddie knows what type of boy you are. You're not fooling anyone with that second-rate acting."

"Two Tony Awards beg to differ," Michael shot back.

"You're not the only one who has had two Tonys . . . except I had mine in my bed, together."

"Ah, Wynny, always with the quick quips. Never a dull moment in those pants."

"I told you never to call me that—I must punish you later for that."

"Promises, promises!"

"Ah, dear boy. I do love the time we spend together."

"And, pray tell, what do you love the most?"

As quick as a flash, she grabbed him by the balls and said with a smile, "The little things."

"What time is your flight tomorrow?" he asked her with a sour look.

"I have a car picking me up at eight; the flight is at ten something, Trans County Airways I think. To think that cheap bastard wouldn't send out the studio jet. I still cannot believe they want *me*, Wynonna Bertrand, to audition. I mean, who the fuck do they think they are? I have a mind to forget it all and tell them to go fuck themselves." she bitched, but privately she thought she'd better not.

"And when will you be back?" he asked, not really listening to her ranting.

"When I decide I've had enough of LA! Oh, dear heart, don't pull that face. I'll call you when I know. Now, let's order, I'll need a large serving of you until I get back. I expect to be filled up, so maybe start with some oysters."

"Followed by a Viagra chaser?"

"If you think you'll need it, then go ahead, my sweet boy, go right ahead."

(2)

THE PRODUCER'S ASSISTANT

Craig Lewis was arriving at JFK after a hectic ride from Manhattan. It never ceased to amaze him no matter what time of the day or night it was, there was always traffic from Manhattan to the airport. He thought of all the limo drivers who had to battle getting their clients to their flights on time. No way would he do it.

He was staying in New York after visiting his parents in Connecticut. His boss, famed producer Jacob Denulle, asked Craig if he would stay on a few days in New York and scope out some places for him. Jacob was interested in making a film with a New York state of mind. Craig would report any places of interest when he got back to LA. Craig was also returning to his boyfriend of four years, celebrity interior designer Patrick Harrington. Around Hollywood, they were known as "the hot couple," a play on words from "the odd couple." They recently purchased a six-bedroom home in Malibu and he couldn't wait to see what Patrick had done with the place.

JFK was mobbed even though it was only 9:10 a.m. *When isn't it mobbed?* he thought. Craig made it through all the check-in and security procedures and was sitting in the Trans County Airways first-class lounge, sipping an orange juice and reading the *New York Times*. He heard a slight commotion at the entrance and looked up to see Hollywood's number-one bitch actress, Wynonna Bertrand, entering with a posse of hangers-on, all making sure every step she took was as comfortable as possible. She was moaning about the trip to the airport and the traffic.

"Why can't this place get a goddamn express route from Midtown to JFK, for fuck's sake?" she screeched so all could here.

God, that woman is crass, thought Craig. *I hope she's not on my flight, but if she is, please don't seat her near me.* He remembered Jacob saying he'd never work with her again after their last encounter. Jacob's favorite saying concerning Ms. Bertrand was, "If that woman was any further up her own cunt, she'd be able to give birth to herself." Jacob could be equally crass.

Craig enjoyed his work and didn't have the usual Hollywood ideas of making it big on his own. He liked Jacob, they worked well together and Jacob was extremely generous when it came to his staff, which was why Craig had just spent four nights at the Four Seasons and was traveling first class. He was only twenty-four, but so far everything had worked out for him. He had a great job, he was in love with a wonderful man and he was moving up in the world—not to mention into a new home. He had a kind of Brad Pitt look about him with his dirty-blond hair. His personality came shining through and he thought his best feature was his eyes, which were hazel and changed color depending on the light. Patrick had told him the first time they met that he was mesmerized by them.

Patrick was twenty-six with fair skin and dark hair, which was so attractive with guys from an Irish background. Patrick was born and raised in the United States after his parents immigrated in the late sixties. He had just finished putting the final touches on their new house, a three-story, six-bedroom, four-bathroom bungalow complete with its own private beach.

Craig made a quick call to Patrick, knowing he would be up even though it was only 6:25 a.m. in LA. Patrick was an early riser and worked out each morning. They spoke for only five minutes, in which Craig said he was due to land in LA just after 1:30 p.m. LA time. He told Patrick he had a car service arranged that would bring him home, so there was no need to pick him up. He also noted that Wynonna Bertrand was at the airport and may be on his flight, which could mean a very long trip home. Patrick told him to ignore her and he added that the house looked fantastic; he was sure Craig would approve. Craig hung up with Patrick, settled back and waited for his flight to be called.

(3)

JENNIFER AND ORLA

"Did you see that guy at breakfast? He had the body of David," said Jen.

"I did. I couldn't concentrate except to ogle him. I think he caught me staring at one stage. And who is this David, by the way? Does Miss Jennifer have a special someone that I don't know about?" Orla replied.

"If I had someone special, I'd hardly be checking other guys out, now, would I? David! You know, the Greek statue? Only this guy was bigger, if you know what I mean. At least, it looked like it from the way his jeans bulged out."

"Oh, Jennifer!"

Jennifer Stone and Orla Finnegan were taking a hotel shuttle to JFK. Both were flight attendants for Trans County Airways and they were due to fly on the New York-Dallas route before finding out they had been changed to the LA nonstop instead. Jen was head flight attendant and would be responsible for a crew of eight, plus her, which was about two short for a normal cross-country flight. Because of the weather down south, they had to make do with whoever was available.

Known as a fair boss, Jen could come down hard if she needed to. At twenty-nine, she came up through the ranks and made head flight attendant about two years ago. Strawberry-blonde hair and green eyes were an unusual combination, but it worked well on her. Jen loved to fly and always had the attention of the male passengers—and on the odd occasion, she was known to have taken one or two home with her. Originally from Maine, Jen was always a popular girl through school and at work. She had no time to settle, she enjoyed the time she spent alone and she only allowed someone else in her life when she desired it. For the last couple of months, however, she had been thinking maybe the time was coming to think about finding the right man, not that she had anyone in mind, but the fellow at breakfast today sure had her attention . . .

Orla Finnegan left her native Ireland four years ago and had been a flight attendant for the past three years. Now twenty-seven, Orla dazzled everyone with her bubbly personality and emerald-green eyes. She was a people person and could make even the most annoyed passenger happy. She had had to deal with some doozies in her time, but schmoozing was her middle name.

Orla was on her last flight before venturing off on yet another exploration. She was never one to sit still and she loved to travel, so working for an airline was a great choice of career for her. Orla was off to Thailand tomorrow for a two-week journey of the country. She had never been there and couldn't wait to arrive. As of this morning, she thought she was doing the New York-Dallas route, which meant she could then transfer to an LA flight, but her boss had just told her they were on the 10:20 a.m. nonstop flight out of JFK to LAX. With her bags already packed for her trip, Orla was quite happy about the last-minute change. She would stay in a hotel close to LAX before flying out at 11:15 a.m. tomorrow. She had done all her research on Thailand and had plans for almost every day, but she had figured in some relaxation time as well.

Upon arriving for the initial preflight checks at the departure gate, Orla nudged Jen in the arm and nodded her head toward the waiting passengers. There, reading a newspaper, was the hunk from breakfast.

"Can you believe our luck? I think I'll imagine him flying on to Thailand and if that's the case, then all my plans are out the window. Hey, a girl can dream, can't she?" Orla said.

Jenny noted he was not waiting in the first-class lounge, so he may be traveling in economy, although not everyone used the first-class lounge. Jen saw some of the other crew arriving but had to wait until the remaining members arrived on a flight from Chicago before she gave her usual preflight briefing. She knew Peter and James were upstairs, so when they turned up, she would get them to make sure the departure desk was set up.

(4)

TWO-GETHER FOREVER

Peter Bailey and James Atkins had arrived early and were just finishing breakfast in the crew lounge. Both were flight attendants, were inseparable and didn't care who knew it. They even took part in a new Trans County Airways advertisement designed to bring in more gay clientele. They had been together since meeting in elementary school and were best friends to start with, but that developed into a strong relationship.

They didn't normally crew the same flights, but they did for the odd occasions when it worked out. Today they would be on the New York-Dallas, Dallas-Miami routes. James was watching the television, which was covering the weather and he noticed that there was some bad weather in the Gulf of Mexico that the announcer was saying could develop into a possible hurricane. He wondered whether this would affect any of their flights today. He wasn't worried; if it did, then the flight would be delayed, cancelled or they could be placed on other routes. He asked Peter to watch while he went to use the bathroom.

Peter Bailey was twenty-four with shaggy blond hair and bright blue eyes; he kind of looked like David Bowie. He had the wow factor big time and everyone commented on him, male and female, gay and straight. Peter grew up in Connecticut and was an A student throughout school. He attended Princeton University and even though he was accepted into Yale, he decided to spend some time out of Connecticut. He adored James, whom he said he fell in love with from the first time they met, even though they were both five at the time. One time while playing, they built forts in the long grass of a vacant lot. It was in one of these forts that Peter and James had their first kiss, at age six. They both knew then that something was right between them; they just did not know what.

James had red hair, gray-green eyes and a swimmer's build. He had been very popular in school and loved his sports. He was at home in the pool and swam laps each morning when time permitted. James was also raised in Connecticut, about forty minutes north of where Peter grew up, but he moved with his family to the same town when he was four and remained there until he graduated and left for the same university as Peter. Together they made a very handsome couple. They now lived just up the road from their families in a nicely renovated three-bedroom cottage overlooking Candlewood Lake, in the town of New Milford.

"That weather in the Gulf is worsening and it's not far away from becoming a category one hurricane," said Peter when James returned.

"Well, I doubt we'll be going to Dallas or Miami. Let's go see what our plans are, or if there have been any changes yet," James replied.

As they walked over to the designated departure gate, they spotted Jennifer Stone, who informed them they had indeed been changed to her nonstop Los Angeles flight. Their original JFK-Dallas flight has been delayed and due to the storm, the Dallas-Miami flight had already been canceled, which in turn delayed some of the original LA flight crew who were due in from Miami using that same aircraft. This came as good news to both Peter and James, because it would be the only flight they would crew today and they would have an afternoon and overnight in Los Angeles. They loved the glitz and glam of LA and were both celebrity junkies.

On top of that, they were assigned to work in the first-class cabin. They both enjoyed working with Jen, who once tried to fix James up with her brother Craig until he explained about Peter.

"Oh my god! Check out the hunk sitting over there," Peter said. He had just spotted Jen and Orla's breakfast babe.

"Wow, an actual god on our flight. Dibs on serving him," said James.

Peter replied, "Hey! Keep it in your pants, sunshine! He's probably traveling coach, so any serving you have in mind will have to be done in your head. Jen just told me we are working with Orla up in first class. And excuse me, sir, but I think you should be more concerned with serving *me*."

"Sorry, mother," James said cheekily.

"Damn, he melts my Ben and Jerry's," he continued.

(5)

PREPARING TO FLY

Jen was waiting for the rest of the cabin crew. Six crew members were arriving on a flight from Chicago, which was due in soon and Jen had to page Adam Richards, who had a day off but said he would work. The crew on the Chicago flight had just called in and were on their way to the departure gate where Jen was waiting. The flight crew would be headed up by Bill Havilland. He liked to go by Billy, which Jen found just a tad precious considering Bill was fifty-four. One thing that put her off were grown men who still use their little-boy names. It was okay if they were under fifteen, but from then on, it should stop. He said his mom always called him that and he just kept it.

Apart from the name, everyone wanted to work with Captain Havilland. He was happily married for thirty years to Sandi and they had three children, two boys and a girl, who were grown and out of the house. Captain Billy was flying the JFK-LAX route round-trip today and would then be taking a few days off to spend some time with Sandi in Vermont.

His copilot was Stuart Orwin and the first officer was Max Alexander. Both had flown with Captain Billy previously and they all got on well together. Stuart and Max had been rumored to get on a little *too* well on occasion; at least, that was the scuttlebutt circulating the rounds at the moment. Nobody knew if either one was gay, straight, or whatever. Both were aware of the rumors but brushed them off with a smile. They certainly spent a lot of time together in and out of the plane, which didn't help curb the gossip seekers; Peter and James were at the head of that line. Besides, there wasn't a flight anywhere in the world that some sort of "who's fucking who" talk wasn't part of the routine.

"It's all a part of being a crew member," said Max, when asked if he was worried about all the innuendos. "I couldn't give a rat's ass what anybody says. It's nobody's business except mine or Stu's and until you hear it from our mouths, then it remains just a rumor, doesn't it?"

There was no gray in Max's life. He saw things purely in black and white and he told it the way it was—absolutely no in-betweens with him. At thirty-six, he did have a certain way about him. He could certainly pass as gay, but there was always that element of doubt surrounding him. His curly hair was always just a tad messy, but he wore his clothes like a catwalk model.

Stuart Orwin grew up one of seven kids and shared a bedroom for his first fifteen years with his older brother, Greg. He was the third oldest of four boys and three girls. Even his own siblings don't know what Stu's deal was. He had never introduced a girl to the family, but he had brought Max home numerous times, saying he was a work friend. He was thirty-four and nobody could pick which side he buttered his bread. He came across as an average guy, someone who you would see in a bar having a drink with his friends, or at home on a football field, but he did have that certain twinkle in his eye around Max.

"Hi, guys," Jen said when the three men arrived.

"Hey, Jen! Are you in charge of the crew for this flight?" Billy asked.

"I sure am, Captain Havilland. I have Orla, Peter and James here so far. I am waiting for the rest of the crew, who have landed, so they should be here shortly. They are coming in on the 9:30 from Chicago and Adam Richards is coming in from home," she told him.

Max did not seem very happy. "Oh great, Peter Bailey and James Atkins. Those two guys are the worst gossips in the world—especially about us. All we have to do is be seen exiting out of the same door and before we know it, we are wrapped up in another crazy sex scandal involving not only the two of us but also a cast of thousands. No, if those guys want to play their little tell-all games, then I think we should at least oblige." He nudged Stu and said, "Want to have a little fun with them, give them something to talk about?"

Stu laughed and said, "Yeah, let's fuck with their heads a bit. By the end of this flight, they may think again about their little storytelling games. I'll get Orla to help; she likes a bit of fun."

Captain Billy grinned but said in a stern voice, "I hope you know what you're doing. You guys are asking for it."

Stu explained that it was just a bit of fun, but he thought, *Those guys have this coming to them. We know what they say behind our backs. We know they would be lost if they didn't have something to say about someone else.*

"Come on, then, let's prepare for the flight," said Captain Billy. He pulled Jen to one side and said, "Just make sure they don't go too far," and then he asked who the other crew were.

"We're waiting on Bryson Williams, Rebecca Lewis, Charlotte Makin and Grace Kemp, who are all coming in from Chicago. Adam Richards has called in and said he is on his way" Jen replied.

"Well, when they've arrived, let me know so I can brief everyone."

"Sure thing, Captain."

Captain Billy thanked Jen and left with Max and Stuart to do the preflight checks. Jen went to make sure the cabin was all in order; while on her way, she asked James and Peter to assist her. Orla waited for the remaining crew to arrive and would then join the others on the plane.

(6)

STORMY WEATHER

"Due to increasing bad weather in the Gulf of Mexico, there will be a delay on arrivals and departures for all Florida, Mississippi, Alabama, Louisiana and Texas flights. Further updates will be advised when the situation becomes clearer," an announcement came over the speaker system throughout the airport.

Instantly passengers departing to those destinations began to mob any airline official, asking a million questions at once. The arrivals area would be equally hectic.

When Orla heard the announcement, she knew what to expect. The fact that she was stationed at the departure desk for an LA flight did not matter to the hoards; as soon as they saw a manned desk, they started their "What do I do? Where do I go? What are you going to do?" questions. Orla simply stated to the gathered crowd, "At the moment it is just a brief delay—it doesn't mean your flights are canceled. The best thing to do is to go to the departure gate for whatever flight you have and wait for further announcements." She soon had the area cleared and got back to business of preparing the desk for the boarding procedure. She noticed the crew from Chicago coming her way, so now it was only Adam she was waiting on. Jen had told her he was on his way, so it wouldn't be much longer before all the crew were here to help out.

Ten minutes later Adam turned up, then Captain Billy gave his briefing. "We have Wynonna Bertrand on board this morning and we have all heard how hard she is to handle. She has two assistants with her, so direct any queries to them—by no means approach Ms. Bertrand directly. I have already heard from the first-class lounge manager that she is in a foul mood, so tread carefully around her. Her assistants have informed Jen that Wynonna wants her area curtained off, which Jen will handle as soon as we have leveled off. Please do not do anything that may upset her and with luck we can have a hassle-free flight. We have done our flight check and it looks like a clear passage through to LA. The plane checked out okay, so we can start boarding as soon as possible. Have a great flight, everyone."

The crew thanked the captain and Jen made her usual preflight speech. "You heard what the captain said. *Do not* piss off Wynonna Bertrand. She is already peeved about something, so I think one of us should be the liaison between Queen Wynonna and her assistants. Orla, do you think you can handle it?"

"Not a problem. She'll be putty in my hands," Orla replied. "Besides, I'm in such a good mood today. After this flight I'm off for two weeks, so not even the Bitch of Hollywood can upset me."

"Let's hope so. We are a bit shorthanded, so Orla, you will be up front with Peter. James and Bryson can do business class; Rebecca, Adam, Charlotte and Grace will be in economy. I will help out wherever I am needed, but you can always ask each other if you think you need help or run out of something. Economy looks packed along with business, but we still have empty seats up in first." Jen went on to tell them to have a safe flight and to make their way to their posts to start the boarding procedure.

Peter saw the reaction on James's face when he was told to work in business instead of in first class. Not that he didn't like working with Bryson—he really didn't know him that well, having only ever worked with him twice before.

Bryson Williams was always dressed immaculately no matter what he was doing. The oldest flight attendant on board at thirty-four, Bryson was a classically good-looking black man with flawless, rich chocolate-brown skin and dark eyes. He was very tall, had played for his college basketball team and was very successful until a knee injury put an end to his career as a pro player. Bryson was well-known for his love of Barry White's music and was always humming or sometimes softly singing a Barry White tune and he did it flawlessly. He was happily married to his wife of six years, LoRayna, who was pregnant and very close to giving birth to their first child. He looked forward to becoming a dad and the crew couldn't be happier for him. They all said he was going to be the best dad a kid ever had.

Peter told James not to worry; he was just a curtain away if he needs anything.

"But what about Wynonna? I wanted to see the diva bitch for myself. I wanted to see if I could get her all riled up, or at least watch and wait until somebody else got a mouthful. You know it's going to happen. Maybe I could throw something at her, like you do at the zoo to get a reaction from the animals," James said.

"I'll let you know if any juicy stuff happens. In the meantime, just chill out," Peter said.

(7)

PLEASE BE SEATED

Jen's voice came over the PA system in the gate area. "Ladies and gentlemen, in a few minutes we will begin the boarding procedure for Trans County Airways Flight 19 to Los Angeles International. We will begin with our first- and business-class passengers, followed by passengers with disabilities and those traveling with children. For those traveling in economy, please take note of your boarding pass. In the bottom right-hand section is a letter from A to F. This will be your designated boarding code. We will be boarding from the rear of the aircraft first and continue forward. Code F is the extreme rear of the aircraft; Code A is the front of economy class. Those traveling in first and business class do not have a code. We will begin boarding shortly."

All the crew were now in place. Peter, Bryson and Orla were at the entrance to the aircraft, ready to greet and direct the boarding passengers. James and Jen were helping the ground personnel at the departure desk in the terminal. Adam, Rebecca, Charlotte and Grace were on board the aircraft doing last-minute checks and making sure everything was secure. They would also assist passengers who needed to find their seats and help with carry-on baggage if needed. The flight crew were in the cockpit doing the preflight checks and paperwork.

The all-clear came over the walkie-talkies and the boarding began. "Ladies and gentlemen, welcome to Trans County Airways

Flight 19, nonstop service from New York to Los Angeles. We will now begin the boarding procedure and we ask you to please have your boarding pass and photo ID ready. First, we would like to call our passengers traveling in first class and business class to make their way to the gate."

Wynonna was flanked by her assistants, Beth Halvison and Michele Stewart. She was ushered onto the aircraft as quickly as possible. Wynonna was pissed she wasn't given priority boarding and had to endure boarding with the commoners. She had a mind to say, "Fuck it all," and go home. She had demanded to board first and to keep anyone away from her. "I'm in no mood for those fucking unwashed autograph junkies. Skuzzy lowlifes," she said.

She could hear the whispers from the waiting passengers. "Did you see who that was?" "She has a mouth on her." "Oh my god, that was Wynonna Bertrand!" "That Wynonna Bertrand is such a bitch."

Craig had left the first-class lounge earlier and was browsing through the stores in the terminal. He made his way to the departure gate slowly and then stood patiently in line behind some other passengers waiting to board. Craig could still hear Wynonna's whining even as she was heading down the jet way. *God, that women is a pain in the world's ass*, he thought. Maybe he would pitch an idea to Jacob about a how a famed Hollywood actress was murdered on a flight.

He noted there were not a lot of people in line for the front end of the plane. That may be a blessing, because Her Royal Highness may keep her fat trap shut for five minutes, though he doubted it.

Economy class looked packed. While waiting in line, Craig was checking out those still seated and noted an extremely handsome man leaning against a column, obviously waiting for his section in economy to be called. The man briefly caught Craig's eye and both men quickly looked away. *Wow, what a looker . . . Hot is not the word,* Craig thought. Craig wasn't checking him out for himself—he didn't need to, with Patrick by his side—but when he saw a beautiful person, be it male or female, on occasion he asked them for their contact details to pass on to Jacob, who was always looking for new talent. This guy had that certain something and was well worth checking out. *By the looks of his jeans, he certainly has a lot to check out,* he thought. If the chance came, he would ask this guy if he would be interested in talking to Jacob. Even if he wasn't, at least he'd get an eyeful.

While Craig was settling into his seat, he took note where Wynonna and her troupe were sitting. She was still ranting about something not being to her liking, but at least she was on the other side of the plane from where he sat. He placed his bag in the overhead compartment and he thought he saw Wynonna looking in his direction. *God, I hope she doesn't recognize me,* he thought.

While in the terminal lounge, he hid behind his newspaper so she wouldn't see him. He remembered the screaming she did while she was on the set of Jacobs's last movie. There was nothing he could do about it now.

The remaining passengers must be aboard by now and Peter came by to make sure he was comfortable. "Not a lot of people in first class today; there are only about eleven passengers. Let me know if there is anything I can get you. Enjoy your flight, sir."

Craig thanked Peter and asked if he knew his sister, Rebecca, because she was a flight attendant with Trans County Airways. "Rebecca Lewis is your sister? She's on the crew for this flight—she's working in economy," Peter explained.

"I didn't know she was on this flight! I was going to give her a call tonight to catch up," Craig said.

"I'll let her know you're up here. I'm sure she'll come up when she gets a chance."

Jen came by to speak with Peter. "All the passengers are now on board, but there looks to be a double booking in economy with one of the passengers. There aren't any spare seats in economy or business, so we're bringing him up here. It's a Mr. Paul Danielson. I think you will approve when you see him."

"If it's the same guy James and I saw in the terminal, then James will be pissed beyond measure, because that guy is yummy," Peter said.

Jen replied, "You'll have some competition with Orla, so be warned. This is the guy who was sitting by us at breakfast and all I can say is oh my god. Which seat shall we put him in?"

Peter briefly looked around and chose an empty seat in the row near Craig. Jen said she would bring him up. Peter could not have been more helpful when he realized it was the same guy he and James had lusted after. He made sure the desirable Mr. Danielson was comfortable.

Craig immediately sat up straight when he saw it was the hunk who was leaning against the column and was now sitting down just on the other side of the aisle. *Maybe this flight will turn out okay after all,* he thought.

(8)

MYSTERY MAN

Paul Danielson must have channeled the actor Bryan Callen in both looks and the way he wore clothes. He was good-looking but didn't throw it in others' faces. Paul was twenty-five and was a manager in the menswear department at Barneys New York. He was still single and not really looking, although quite a few coworkers and customers would like to get to know him intimately.

Paul grew up with his parents and his three siblings, all adopted, because the Danielson's were unable to conceive. They lived in a very happy and unregimented home in rural Kentucky. He did well at school but didn't want to take it any further, so he never did any university studies or the like. He wanted to be a singer, but unfortunately he was not blessed with much talent in that department; after a few auditions he was told his looks were not enough. Once out of school, he did make one attempt to further this education, trying his luck studying journalism, but after a trip to New York City when he was nineteen, he stumbled into a sales position at Barneys—literally.

During that trip, he and a buddy went into Barneys because they had heard all about it and wanted to see for themselves. They had no idea it was so swanky and expensive. Even the restaurant was over the top. Paul picked up a T-shirt and immediately put it back when he read the $150 price tag. Paul was tapped on the shoulder and the salesman asked if he needed any help. This made him jump back and he fell over the guy. Neither was injured and they both had a laugh about it. It turned out it was the sales manager, John Watkins and he asked Paul if he lived in New York or was just visiting. After explaining he was attempting a move to New York if he could find work, John asked Paul if he would be interested in a job at Barneys. Not having any luck with the job search so far, Paul decided to give it a try.

It meant finding a place to stay in New York City, which was not the easiest thing to do. Paul asked his buddy, Roy Higgins, if he would also like to try his luck in the city and both guys made the move. They found a fourth-floor walk-up on West Seventy-Ninth Street near Riverside Drive. The place was affordable, especially because Roy was also offered a position at Barneys, albeit in the receiving department and only part-time. That was okay, because Roy had stars in his eyes and wanted to try acting. He also needed more time for the many women he bedded. He seemed to bring home a different one almost every night and then tell Paul all the nasty details. Roy joined a theater group and got a few bit parts, but the group director said it wouldn't be long before he had a lead role.

Paul found his niche at Barneys and was elevated into being a buyer after about two years on the floor. After a few more years he made sales manager in the menswear department, after John left for greener pastures. Things were starting to look up for both Paul and Roy. Their move to the city was paying off, with Paul now sales manager and as promised Roy got his lead role. A talent scout saw Roy and signed him for a Broadway production, which was to begin in a few months. With the new fortunes, both guys decided to move up in the world and find a better apartment. They found a great sixth-floor, two-bedroom apartment in a doorman building on West Forty-Ninth, between Ninth and Tenth Avenues.

Paul purchased a top-of-the-line computer and became an Internet junkie. With his newfound prowess on the computer, Paul began to do some investigative work and attempted to find out who his birth parents were. After quite some time, he discovered his mother's name was but had no luck with his father. Further investigation bought more light about who his mother was and the information was quite eye-opening to Paul. This latest bit of information made him realize why people always said he looked familiar.

He had phone numbers and an address, so he made the decision to contact her to see if she was interested in meeting him. After receiving no answer to any of his phone calls, he decided to pay a visit to the only address he was able to acquire. The address was in New York City, as luck would have it, but he had no luck when he knocked on the door. He went back a few hours later; this time the door opened and he knew he had found his mother. The woman asked him into the house and they sat in the living room while Paul spoke. At first the lady was taken aback by his story and seemed to soften a little, but in a classic Jekyll and Hyde moment she changed tack and told him she didn't want anything to do with him and she asked him to leave her house and to never contact her again. She said if he did, she would make his life hell.

Paul was stunned by the lack of feeling this woman showed. *How could anyone not want to know her own child?* he thought.

Once out on the street, he went from bewildered to anger and decided then and there to get himself some revenge. If she didn't want him around, then that was exactly what she would get. *Ms. Wynonna Bertrand, it was time to play the role of victim. You don't know what hell is,* he thought.

Paul never mentioned to Roy or anybody else about attempting to find his birth parents, or going to see his mother. He wanted to see how this would pan out before telling anybody. He also didn't want to upset his adopted family if this was all a big mistake. Knowing his mother was a big Hollywood star was a massive piece of information to reveal, so he thought it was best to keep it under wraps for now.

As time went on, Paul's anger toward Wynonna became obsessive and he plotted her murder with meticulous detail. He didn't want to do anything in New York; he wanted to do it well away from his home and life. He bided his time and after checking out Wynonna's Facebook page, he discovered her need to fly to California to audition for a movie. He knew this was the best opportunity to carry out his revenge on her. It was the perfect location and her reputation as a hard-ass pain in the neck—and the fact it was well documented that a lot of people in Hollywood wanted her silenced—was a bonus. Wynonna revealed when she was going and even the airline and time details. For some reason Wynonna thought her fans needed to know this information, but nobody really cared. For someone who hated the public, she sure went to extremes to make sure she was surrounded by them. *Ego-loving whore,* he thought.

Paul made his plans and to all he told, he sounded like he was taking a regular vacation to Los Angeles. Roy said he wanted to go, but his play was about to begin, so he remained behind. Paul was relieved because he didn't want anyone around. This was going to be a trip of a lifetime that would change Paul's life forever—he was going to make sure of that.

(9)

THE IN-FLIGHT ENTERTAINMENT

In economy, the crew was getting ready for takeoff by making sure everyone was seated, including the usual roundup of wayward children whose parents seemed to think it was the cabin crew's job to look after their kids for them. Rebecca had to twice ask a couple to keep their children seated or risk being asked to leave the aircraft. It never ceased to amaze her how many parents let their kids run around a plane without care. Two passengers, Millicent DeBarge and Thelma Jackson, were large black women from New Jersey on their way to California for a vacation. They didn't hold back when some snot-nosed brats came running up the aisle and started bickering near them.

"Where's your momma at?" Thelma asked them, but they ignored her. She turned toward the back of the plane and yelled, "Whoever in charge of these youngin's better keep them in check and out of my face, or else ya'll going to have to deal with me. Best come up here and put them on a leash or somethin', or else they gonna end up in one of these overhead bins here." One mother came forward and dragged the two kids back to their seats, all the while threatening them with all types of punishment.

Both ladies were entertaining those passengers seated around them with their chatter. When Bryson walked through the cabin from business class to chat with Adam, Millicent started with some humorous flirting. "Mmm mmm, check out that tall drink of Coca-Cola. Hoo, child, he can fly me anytime," she said.

"Millie, hush now; don't be embarrassing me. That boy is just doin' his job and don't need you all down his stuff," retorted Thelma.

Millie replied, "Down his stuff? Mmm *mmm*, girl, let me take that all in now. All I can say is he doin' a fine job imitating John Wayne, goin' by that piece he's carryin' up front. Who you kiddin', girl? Don't be tellin' me you weren't checkin' out that fine chocolate éclair yourself! I'm just waitin' till that boy comes back through here, so I can check out that sweet Georgia peach he calls an ass. You know the Lord was havin' a good day when he created that."

"Oh, hush up now. You are bad, but you're right, girl—that boy brings my kettle to boil. He can dip his teabag in my pot anytime," agreed Thelma.

"Ooh, you bad, but you ain't lyin' girl. I hear ya!" Millie said.

Everyone around them was in tears with laughter, including some of the flight crew. A recently returning Bryson was softly singing, "I'm never goin' to give you up, I'm never ever goin' to stop . . ." He gave the ladies a small wiggle of his rear end as he returned through the business-class curtain, much to Millie's and Thelma's delight. Both let out a loud whoop to signal their pleasure.

The aircraft began to move backward from the gate. Craig could see the ground crew out of his window and thought the guy using the tractor to push the aircraft looked kind of cute. He was distracted by Jen's voice coming over the PA system. The flight crew was about to perform the usual preflight instructions about exits, seat belts and life vests. Not everyone was reading the aircraft instruction card like they should be, Thelma and Millicent noted loudly. They gave 100 percent attention to the crew as Jen explained about the floor lighting and seat belts. They were most interested when Jen announced there would be a light snack and a lunch served during the flight.

"All right, now that's what I want to hear. I hope they have something good to eat, cause I'm starved," said Thelma.

"Don't be expectin' no fried chicken and black-eyed peas, now. It'll most probably be a sandwich or somethin'," replied Millie.

"I hear they got wine and beer as well," said Thelma.

"Don't you be getting all liquored up and make me have to hold your sorry ass up. You stick to water!" Millie scolded.

"Water? I may be a jewel, but I ain't no goldfish."

Next on the PA system came Captain Billy's voice, asking the flight crew to cross-check and prepare for takeoff. The flight crew replaced all the instructional items and sat down. By this time, the plane was just about to make the turn onto the runway. Once again Captain Billy's voice came over the PA, telling the passengers that they were next in line for takeoff and it wouldn't be too long. It took about three minutes before the plane began the turn onto the runway and the usual sound of the jet engines began to roar, signaling they were taking off.

Millie hung on to Thelma for dear life and did not make a sound; this was Millie's first flight but Thelma had flown once before, to her son in Atlanta. With that one flight under her belt, she thought she was a frequent flier and she took it upon herself to reassure Millie that all was okay and that everything was normal.

"What-choo talkin' about? You flew one time and now you tellin' me like you ready to be a pilot or something!" Millie screamed.

All Thelma did was hold up her hands, as if to say, "Whatever, but at least I've flown before."

Millie began to relax and was watching New York grow smaller and smaller. It was a clear day, so the landscape was visible as the jet flew out over Rockaway Bay and began to turn toward the west, past the city and over New Jersey. She could see Manhattan in the distance and asked Thelma if she thought they would be able to see their houses in Trenton. Thelma rolled her eyes at Millie, who didn't see because she had returned to looking out the window.

Captain Billy made yet another announcement. "Good morning, everybody. This is your captain speaking. My name is Billy Havilland, your copilot is Stuart Orwin, and the first officer is Max Alexander. We would like to welcome you to Trans County Airways Flight 19 from New York's JFK Airport, nonstop to Los Angeles.

The flight time will be approximately five hours and forty-five minutes and we expect a smooth, clear flight for you today. We will be flying at thirty-five thousand feet and once we have leveled out, I will be turning off the 'fasten seat belt' sign and you will be allowed to move about the cabin, however while you are seated, it is always best to have your seat belt fastened. Your flight crew is headed up by Jennifer Stone, who along with the rest of the crew will make sure they will make your flight as comfortable as possible. Please do not hesitate to ask for any assistance if you need it. The flight crew will be serving drinks shortly, along with a light snack and as Jen said, there will be a lunch served later in the flight. Once again, thank you for flying with Trans County Airways. Enjoy your flight."

(10)

THELMA AND MILLICENT

Thelma Fuller grew up in the Atlanta suburbs. Not one to stand by while the world walked all over her, she did quite well at school and was one of only a few from her school to graduate and go on to college. She met and fell in love with Henry Jackson, marrying him when she turned twenty. Henry was two years her senior and had already been working in the factory since he left school at seventeen. The Jacksons made a home for themselves not far from where Thelma grew up and it wasn't too long before their first child appeared. Travis Jackson took after his mother and was academically gifted. Their two other children, Sharlene and William, didn't do so well at school. William, or Bubba as he was known, left school at fifteen and began to work with his father. Sharlene left school at sixteen and found part-time work at a local hair salon. She started as a cleanup girl but trained after-hours in the art of hair styling and she was now quite well-known around town for her inventive designs; she and her husband now own the salon. Travis left Atlanta when he was nineteen and moved to New Orleans with his girlfriend. Henry had an opportunity to move to New Jersey to be a foreman; he and Thelma moved house to Trenton and this was where Thelma first met Millie.

Millicent Hunting was born and raised in Trenton. She plodded through school and only ever wanted to be a housewife and look after her husband and family. She met George DeBarge when she was eighteen and married him at nineteen. By twenty she had her first of five children. She lived a poor but happy life doing the best she could with the little money George earned. George found work at the local plastics factory and was able to work his way up to the position of supervisor. George met Henry Jackson when Henry was brought in to be foreman; they hit it off and became close friends. The families met and Thelma and Millie became best friends.

Now in their sixties and with both husbands retired, they were free to do what they pleased. They recently decided to take a trip together—not their usual drive to the country, but a real trip. Thelma had to convince Millie to fly and it didn't take long for them to settle on Los Angeles.

"We need to see where those stars put their feet and hands in the cement. I'm dyin' to stand on Mr. Billy Dee Williams's shoe prints. I don't even know if he has any shoe prints there, but that man makes my heart stop and turn back time," Thelma said.

"I want to go see the homes of all those stars. We can take one of those bus tours I keep hearin' about. Hey, maybe we can get onto a show or something, maybe see Ellen and get us some of those prizes she keeps given out," Millie said excitedly.

"We can try, 'cept I don't know how we can do it. Maybe we can ask when we get there at the hotel or something."

They planned this trip for months, debating where to stay and what to do, adding this and removing that, along with many arguments and name-calling. They eventually decided on a date and would spend one week out in LA taking in all the tourist spots they had always heard about.

"They got something called the La Brea Tar Pits out there. Maybe we'll check out that", Thelma suggested.

"I ain't goin' all the way to Los Angeles to see no god-damn tar pit. I get enough thick black crap here with ol' molasses ass over there sittin' around all day," Millie replied, referring to her husband, George.

They chose a hotel central to everything but not in a bad neighborhood. They got a flight that was nonstop because this was Millie's first attempt at flying anywhere, so the less takeoffs and landings, the better. They gave the details to a local travel agent, who set them up with everything they needed to make a wonderful trip. Henry and Thelma drove to pick up Millie and George so they could all go to the airport and so the men can make sure their wives left. George and Henry told them not to worry about anything, have a great time and bring them back a souvenir. Thelma and Millie told both men not to burn down the house and make sure they ate. They were now seated comfortably on board and waiting to take off on their first real adventure together.

(11)

THE CREW

Once the plane started to level out, the flight crew readied the beverage carts so they could start the drink and snack service. Adam, Grace and Charlotte were in the galley at the back of the plane to serve those in economy class. Rebecca said she was going to say a quick hello to her brother and would be right back.

Grace asked if the others saw the creepy, skinny man and woman in row forty-six. "Both of them look like they need to be fed badly. They keep looking down and just give me the creeps."

Charlotte said she noticed them but didn't think anything about them; she just thought they looked scared or something. Grace advised it might be an idea to keep an eye on them, though it was just a feeling.

Charlotte asked, "Did you hear those two ladies up the front? They had the cabin in stitches."

Adam said, "They were so funny. It's going to be a fun flight up there."

By this time Rebecca had returned and joined in, saying both women were too much. Grace wasn't nearby when Millie and Thelma had put on their show, so had to be filled in on what went down. She told the others to come and get her if they started up again.

Grace Kemp was always one to notice the crazies because she had an incident about four years ago on a flight to Honolulu. Once again, a creepy-looking person started a weird conversation with her, which made her uncomfortable and when the plane landed, he asked her to his hotel room. He even followed her out of the airport. She had to call another male flight attendant to help her. An intense argument took place and then the person took off. Grace was thirty-one and had been with Trans County Airways for twelve years. She was a senior flight attendant and was usually the boss on her flights, but because of the last-minute changes in New York, she let Jen take the reins on this flight. Grace had the most fantastic hair, which was an unusual color: brassy and sometimes a rich red with gold highlights; it all depended on the light. Her emerald eyes matched her hair perfectly. She had been married for the past five years, which was a rarity when it came to flight attendants. Grace was seriously thinking about starting a family with her husband, Kane, whom she had met at a staff get-together. He worked in the maintenance facility at JFK for Trans County Airways.

Charlotte Makin was a little sassy black woman, only five foot one, but she could talk the ear off of anyone. At twenty-three, she had just started her career in the airline industry and so far she was having the time of her life. Not one to shy away from the norm, Charlotte sported an Afro hairdo that came straight out of the seventies, but it suited her so well. Her big brown eyes and sweet face was almost pixyish, but it all worked together. She had an ample bosom, which she used to her advantage. With no one in her life, she was a free spirit and loved to tell her life story to anyone who would listen. Charlotte said she had to go and check out the weirdos one more time. She'd report back to the others with her opinion, which both Rebecca and Grace knew would be colorful. Charlotte had a not-so-hidden agenda on this flight. She had her eyes, boobs and (if she had her way) legs open for Adam. She said it was her destiny to bed that boy.

Rebecca Lewis, like Charlotte, was just starting out. She was the youngest of five siblings and at twenty-two she was still at home but knew it wouldn't be long before she had a place of her own. Rebecca had three brothers and a sister, but she was closest to her brother Craig. Rebecca always teased Craig about being a famous

Hollywood producer's assistant and kept asking to spill all the beans on the Hollywood elite. He never would. She thought about making her home near him in California, which would work out great, because she adored Patrick, her brother's lover.

Both Rebecca and Craig looked alike, right down to their dirty-blond hair and hazel eyes. The other Lewis children all shared the hazel eyes, but two had dark brown hair and their older sister, Elaine, had red hair. Rebecca found out that Craig was on this flight up in first class and was delighted. She knew Craig would ask her stay at the new place when she told him her next flight wasn't for another two days. Of course she would accept, because both boys always treated her like a queen—plus she was dying to see the new place they had just purchased. Rebecca could also bend the guys' ears about possibly renting a place close by.

She made her way up to first class, found Craig and briefly told him they would catch up when they landed, because she didn't think she would be able to chat too much during the flight; economy class was packed. If she could get a few moments, she would try to come back. As she left, Craig said, "Don't forget, you'll be staying with us, okay?" Her smile told him it was more than okay and she gave him a little wave.

All the female flight attendants wanted to work with Adam Richards and most wanted to go to bed with him. He was the most handsome guy they had met. Adam was often stopped in the streets and asked for an autograph because of his movie-star looks. He had an extremely quiet nature, which made him even more desirable. When he smiled, the girls melted at his feet. Even though he came across as quiet and shy, he had a wicked sense of humor and could tell the filthiest jokes. No one on board had dated him and so once again the rumor mill was spinning. The current rumor was that Adam was excellent in bed and was very well endowed and straight—a rarity in male flight attendants. Adam had an identical twin brother back home in New York and like most twins they are extremely close. His brother, Tom, is a carpenter with his own business, and is gay. For a while their parents thought both boys were gay because they only ever brought home male friends. Then

Adam went to college and brought a girl home to meet them. That relationship didn't work out, but he has had many others. Being identical, they both had curly ash-brown hair and green eyes deeply set into a chiseled face. Even today they could still fool their parents into thinking one was the other.

Charlotte told Grace she had her eyes on Adam and she wouldn't rest until she had him in her grasp. She demonstrated the last comment while holding a banana. Grace was the motherly type and told Charlotte not to upset him; if he gave her the brush off, then she should let it go.

"Huh! I don't think so. I'm getting a vibe from that boy, so I'm going for it. Besides, I need to see for myself if all those rumors are true. Not to mention that boy is fine with a capital F," Charlotte replied.

It didn't take long for her to get her chance, because when Grace left the galley, Adam walked in and asked Charlotte what she was up to tonight. She told him she had nothing planned. He then said, "Want to grab something to eat and hang out?"

Charlotte replied in her usual forward way. "I'd grab whatever you're hanging out, baby!"

He smiled his devil smile, laughed and said they could talk later, but she shouldn't lose that train of thought. He went out into the cabin while Charlotte watched him. She knew then that tonight was going to be the night she could lay all those rumors to bed by laying with one Adam Richards.

(12)

DRINKS, ANYONE?

The four attendants in economy went out into the cabin to start the drink service, two in each row. In business class, James and Bryson had to work a row by themselves, with Jen helping out when she could. By comparison, first class was a doddle, with each passenger being served personally by Peter and Orla, who brought each order on a silver platter like a waiter. Unlike those seated in economy, first-class passengers had more of a choice than a lousy pack of peanuts. On offer was a variety of cakes and desserts and a complimentary bar including champagne, coffee and a selection of teas from around the world. Peter and Orla even had napkins draped over their forearms.

Peter was serving Craig, who kept looking at him a little harder than he normally would. "This sounds like some sort of come-on, but I think I know you; I just can't remember from where. You look very familiar," Craig said.

Peter replied, "I was thinking the same thing. My name is Peter Bailey, if that rings a bell."

"I remember you! I'm Craig Lewis. You used to live in Connecticut. I went to New Milford High and you went to Brookfield High. We competed against each other at a couple of swim meets," Craig said excitedly.

"Oh my god! How are you? I remember you too. I still live there, as a matter of fact. You were a quick swimmer, as I remember it—a champion as well," Peter said.

"Still am. Well, not the champion part, but I swim every day when I can. Tell me, what have you been up to?" Craig asked.

"Let me get the drinks out of the way and I'll come back and we can catch up. There aren't that many passengers up here, so I won't be long. I can't wait to hear what you have been doing."

Craig heard Peter ask the hunky guy across the way what he would like. Craig wanted to hear the man's voice, just to see if he was someone Jacob might be interested in. Having a great voice was a big plus with Jacob. Paul did not disappoint: he had an extremely sexy voice with a hint of a southern accent, which matched his good looks. He kind of looked like a movie star—in fact, Craig thought he'd seen that face in the movies somewhere before.

Soon enough Peter had served the remaining passengers. Orla was dealing with Wynonna and her assistants, plus a few other passengers behind them.

"Hi again," Peter said.

"Hey, Peter," Craig replied.

Peter sat down in the empty seat in front of Craig, which could swing around. Sometimes people did that to have business meetings.

"So what have you been up to?" Peter asked.

Craig regaled Peter with what had happened since high school, starting with his university days and working up to the present position he had with Jacob. He also mentioned his relationship with Patrick and spoke about how proud he was of him and their life in California. Peter was delighted to hear Craig was gay, because he could open up about his relationship with James. He asked Craig if he remembered James in school.

Craig said he vaguely remembered the name. "Did he have red hair?"

"That's him, James Atkins," Peter said. "Do you want to say hello? He's in business class and would love to see you again."

"Really? Wow, I'd love to see him again. This is fantastic, although there is something I should tell you. It's kind of silly. I had a huge crush on him when I saw him at the swim meets," Craig admitted.

Peter laughed and said, "He'll love to hear that! You *have* to tell him. If you don't, I will."

"You don't play fair." Craig laughed.

"As soon as I get a chance, I'll go and see if he can come up. He's probably in the middle of doing the drink service, so it may be a while. I'll finish up here and come back with James," Peter said. He then went and served Paul, who Craig had noticed ordered a coffee drink along with what looked to be chocolate mousse. Peter handed Paul a crisp white linen napkin in which two spoons were wrapped. *Damn, that guy is attractive—a real Hollywood face,* thought Craig.

While Peter was gone, Craig heard Wynonna bitch at one of her assistants.

"Oh, sit down, you stupid fool of a girl. I'm just stretching my legs," she told the assistant, who had jumped up as soon as she saw Wynonna had moved. "Make sure there is a Scotch on ice here when I get back. Do you think you can handle that, or do I need to write it down?"

Craig caught all the commotion and quickly looked around for a magazine to hide behind, but it was too late—she was coming his way.

"Don't you work for Jacob Danulle?" she asked him.

"That's right. I'm his assistant, Craig Lewis," he replied.

"You know, I heard what he has been saying about me, so you can go back to that piece-of-shit, no-talent boss of yours and tell him Wynonna Bertrand says if his cock was any further up his own ass, the only way he could cum would be through his mouth. You can also tell him to go fuck himself." With that, she marched back toward her seat and barked to her assistants. "Make sure I have *complete* privacy. It will be your job if anyone disturbs me."

Craig was stunned but not surprised. He had heard that Wynonna was out for Jacobs's blood after his remarks about her had made the tabloids. One thing he was sure of: he would not repeat what she said about Jacob. He'd find out eventually; Hollywood was not known for having discrete residents.

He then saw Orla with Jen, who had arrived from helping in business class and they drew the curtains surrounding not only Wynonna's seat but those around her she requested be kept vacant, making a small private room of sorts.

"This should make you more comfortable, Ms. Bertrand," said Orla.

"I'll be the judge of that. If anybody disturbs me, I'll personally make sure you're fired. You'll never work again. Do you understand me?"

"I'll do my utmost to make sure nobody disturbs you, Ms. Bertrand. In fact, I'll keep myself close by at all times, to keep everyone away," Orla told her.

Jen and Orla moved away to speak.

"How can you let her talk to you like that? Do you want me to have a word with her?" Jen asked.

Orla replied, "It doesn't bother me. She's just being the diva she thinks the public expects her to be. Miserable old cow."

"Don't you believe it," one of Wynonna's assistants, Beth, said. She was nearby and overheard Jen and Orla. "This is her normal, everyday treatment that she dishes out to anyone and everyone. Actually, that was tame for her—she must have been holding back."

"My god, how do you stand working for her?" they asked.

"It's hard, but if my plans work out, I can be rid of her for good. I will admit there are times when I feel like taking a knife to that throat, just to shut it up. I know that's a horrible thing to say, but I'm not the only one to think it—Michele over there thinks the same way, as do all her staff. We sometimes sit around and discuss the best way to do it. Her personal chef said he'd happily supply the knife." She pointed to where Wynonna's other assistant was sitting reading a magazine.

"Wow, just keep that a thought and not an action until the flight is over. That's the last thing we need, a dead diva," Jen told her jokingly. Paul was in earshot of this conversation and tried very hard to conceal the look of interest, not to mention the satisfaction on his face.

(13)

REUNITED...
AND IT FEELS SO GOOD!

It took about fifteen minutes before Peter returned with James. After James and Craig were reunited, Peter gave Craig a knowing look and said, "Isn't there something you wanted to tell James?"

"Uh, no, I don't think so," Craig replied with a nasty look at Peter.

"What did you want to tell me?" James asked him.

"No, I can't—it's too embarrassing. Ask Peter and he'll fill you in."

Peter interrupted and said, "Oh no, you don't. You said you would tell him, so come on. It's not that bad, for goodness sake and besides, it was eight years ago."

"Well somebody tell me or I'll burst!" James said.

Craig swallowed hard and told James, "I kind of had a crush on you when we swam meets together."

"You did? How sweet of you to say," James replied.

"Of course I had no idea about the two of you, so I'm glad I didn't take it any further. How embarrassing would that have been?" Craig said.

"Well, now I feel great. It's always a nice feeling, to hear someone admires you," James said. "What exactly did you like?"

"Oh no, that would be way too embarrassing," Craig said, blushing.

"Oh, don't be silly. We have just met up after eight years. I want to know. You know I'm not going to stop harassing you until you tell me!"

Craig realized they were not going to let him get out of it, so he said, "Okay, to be honest, I thought you had the sexiest body I had ever seen and when you took your shorts off at the pool to reveal your lime-green Speedo, I had to jump in the pool so no one could see . . . well, let's just say my attraction to you. There, now you know." Craig was bright red.

Peter was grinning from ear to ear, as was James. James said to Craig, "Thank you and do not be embarrassed. I'll tell you in front of Peter, I noticed you as well. And just so you know I'm not just saying it—I remember you because you used to wear a white Speedo, am I right?"

"You are and I still do, although not the same pair. That would be gross. Thank you for remembering that," Craig said, feeling a bit more relaxed.

"God, get a room, will you?" Peter said. He was almost laughing. "I notice neither of you mentioned me in your little reminiscence."

James and Craig both said together, "Black Speedos," and they laughed as Peter touched his hand to his heart in his best Scarlett O'Hara pose.

He said. "Oh fiddle-dee-dee." Then in a normal tone he added, "You know, it does feel good."

Peter said both he and James had to go prepare for the lunch service, but they could do some more catching up after that was over. James went back to business class and left Peter to what he described as "the first-class la-dee-da service."

"It was great seeing the both of you again and I couldn't be more happier to see you two together," Craig said.

"It's great, isn't it? I know James will be bending Bryson's ear in business class, regaling about a long-lost friend from our school days who has come back into his life. Poor Bryson, I say," Peter said with a grin.

"Who is Bryson?" Craig asked.

"The other flight attendant in business class," Peter replied.

Craig nodded. Peter then asked him what his choice for lunch was. Craig had perused the menu earlier and had already chosen the split-pea soup and roast chicken with vegetables. He decided against a dessert even though they all sounded divine; instead he settled for a piece of fruit.

"I need to go and prepare the lunch trays. I'll be back and we can chat again later," Peter said.

Craig settled down with a magazine and decided it may be a good time to have a chat with the dishy Mr. Danielson.

(14)

AT YOUR SERVICE

Wynonna's dulcet tones emanated from behind her curtained seat. She could hear Beth and Michele chatting about this and that. "If one of you could take the time out of your busy, extremely boring, 'don't do anything except piss me off' lives, I desire a drink. Think you could handle that? I am not paying you to sit around discussing hair color, you know. You're here to serve me. Get me a Scotch with ice—now!"

Michele rolled her eyes. The fact was Wynonna Bertrand did not pay for them to wait on her—Wynonna did not pay for anything if she didn't need to, because Beth and Michele were employed by Wynonna's management and not by her. Michele went to arrange the drink and found Peter, who said he would take it to her.

"Thank you. I have had enough of that woman. If I don't quit by the time this plane lands, then I'll be up for murder. With luck, she'll have enough Scotch to put her out for a few hours; that's what usually happens. She's an old soak," Michele said.

When Peter brought Wynonna her drink, she quickly downed it and demanded another. He left to bring her another and made sure there was enough Scotch in first class to hold out. Wynonna had a reputation for drinking excessively; she never appeared drunk in public, though. Who knew how much that woman was going to have? Luckily enough, there were three bottles in the galley.

Rebecca told Adam she would be right back; she wanted to go up and see her brother. She said she'd be about ten minutes. Adam didn't mind. He was on his way out into the cabin with some drinks for a couple of passengers. Rebecca made her way to Craig, who was chatting with Peter.

"Hey, guys. I took a quick break to come up and see you. Economy is packed, but this crowd isn't too demanding and is mainly quiet, so I thought I'd take the opportunity. How are things up here?"

Peter replied that all was well. Wynonna was having a bitch session every now and then, but nothing over the top. He said he would leave them to chat.

Craig told Rebecca about the trip home and the places he saw in New York that he thought Jacob might like to use in his next film.

"Do you and Patrick have any plans tonight?" Rebecca asked.

"Well, seeing as you are staying with us, whatever plans we have, you will be a part of—but at the moment, I don't think we have. I'm going to ask Peter and James if they want to have dinner someplace. Maybe we can have dinner on board the *Queen Mary*; they would love that. It all depends on Patrick and whether he has to work or has made other arrangements. He didn't mention anything when I called him from the airport. Then again, he doesn't know I'll be bringing his favorite sister-in-law home as a surprise, either. Not that he'd mind—he adores you," Craig said.

"Yay! I can't wait to see him again and the new place. I've got something I want to discuss with you and Patrick. I had better get back to work. I'll try to come up and see you again; otherwise, I'll see you when we land."

Rebecca made her way back to economy. On the way, she passed Bryson, who asked if she would help with an elderly female passenger. "The old girl just needs some assistance getting down the aisle, nothing else."

Rebecca said no problem and as soon as she had the elderly passenger back in her seat, she returned to prepare for the lunch service.

(15)

JOIN THE CLUB

Grace was not looking forward to serving her creepy couple, but she soon learned they weren't so bad, just a bit apprehensive about flying. She found out it was their first time going anywhere away from their hometown of Greenville, in upstate New York. They had won a competition that their son had entered them in and were now on their way for a two-week, all-expenses-paid trip featuring Disneyland and everything Hollywood. Earlier, Grace had looked up the passenger manifest and found out their names were Norman and Katherine Great.

Calling them by their names seemed to calm them a little and they told her they were looking forward to seeing the stars on the Hollywood Walk of Fame and Grauman's Chinese Theater and they had plans to buy lots of souvenirs. Grace asked if they were looking forward to Disneyland, but they said they didn't know what to expect when they got there. All they said was they were excited about the fireworks that supposedly happened at 9:00 p.m. each night. They had plans to see them every night without fail. Grace told them that it all sounded like a great adventure and she said if there was anything they needed, all they had to do was ask. She decided to add some extra cookies with their after lunch coffee.

Grace then returned to the galley to find Adam and Rebecca chatting. Grace told them she was very wrong about the couple in row forty-six. "They are so sweet and they look so out of place. I think I will make up a bag of goodies to hand to them before we land." Both Rebecca and Adam thought that was a great idea.

Opposite Norman and Katherine sat Anna Barstow and Owen Michaels. Both attended UCLA and were destined for the high life. They were the type of people who liked to cause a stir, very political in their views. They both wanted to help those who needed it most: gay rights, the right to choose, save the whales and more—whatever the cause of the day was, Anna and Owen were there to lend a hand.

They met while attending yet another rally and decided then and there to make a life with one another. Quite hippy in looks, Owen had a ponytail and wore tie-dyed T-shirts. Anna liked the wild hair, no-makeup, farmer's wife look. Both carried backpacks when they traveled; they were returning home after a human rights rally in New York. Anna was reading her book while Owen was slyly copping a feel of Anna's left breast. It looked like he was leaning over to see what she was reading but his left arm was extended across his body while his fingers played around with her nipple.

"Feel like seeing if the club is opened?" he asked.

"Really, you want to? I could use some stimulation of the Owen kind. We'll go together, but make sure nobody is around before you enter," she replied with a smile.

"Depends on where you want to be entered. If anyone is around, maybe I'll invite him or her in, if you know what I mean . . . Right, let's go. I'm right behind you literally," Owen said.

Little did they know that Katherine Great heard most of what they were saying. "Norman, did you hear that couple? They said there is a club on board! I wonder what sort of club it is? Maybe there are prizes or something, or maybe it's like a bridge club. Next time the stewardess comes by, let's ask her if we can join. I hope it is a bridge club—you know how good I am," she said excitedly.

"I know, honey. You are the best bridge player in the whole of Greenville. Nobody at church can beat you, that's for sure," Norman said proudly.

Katherine looked around to see Anna walking into one of the toilets while Owen waited outside looking a little flushed in the face. She thought they were using the bathroom on their way to the club, which must be down the back of the plane. She didn't think any more about it until Grace came by.

After getting Grace's attention, Katherine asked, "Sorry to bother you, but the two people sitting across from us were talking about a club on board and we were wondering what the club was and how we could join."

Grace replied with a confused look, "I'm not sure what they must have been talking about. We don't have any clubs on board. Are you sure that's what they said?"

"Well, I heard the man ask the lady if she felt like seeing if the club was open and then they headed down the back. I saw her go into the bathroom and he was waiting for her. I didn't see anything after that, but I assume they went to this club thing," Katherine told her.

After hearing Katherine's version of events, it dawned on Grace what Anna and Owen must have been saying and what they were up to. She said she would be right back. Grace made her way to the galley area to find Charlotte and Rebecca chatting while arranging some carts.

"Oh my god, oh my god, oh my fucking god! My two first-time fliers, Norman and Katherine, just asked me if they can join the club we have on board," Grace said with a laugh.

"What club?" Rebecca and Charlotte said in unison.

"Katherine overheard the couple alongside say they were going to the club and she saw them head for the bathroom. They meant the mile-high club and Katherine wants to join. She thinks it's a bridge club or something. What do I tell them?" Grace said in a panicked tone, "Shit, shit, shit, shit."

Charlotte could not stop laughing while Rebecca was trying to think of a believable explanation to tell the Greats. "Tell them that the club is only for frequent fliers or something, or tell them the club isn't opened on this flight. You'll have to think up something before the other couple returns, because you know the Greats will quiz them on this so-called club. You may have to intercept the other couple and explain it to them, but that will mean they'll know that you know. Oh god, it's a huge mess," Rebecca said.

"I know—I'll try the frequent-flier thing; that sounds kind of logical," Grace replied.

Grace returned to the cabin to see the "club couple" returning to their seats and Katherine Great leaning across to speak to the woman. *Fuck, fuck, fuck, too late,* she thought. Then she grinned as she thought that fucking was probably the subject they were discussing at this very moment. *Whatever these people are saying to poor, naive Katherine Great, I guess I'll soon find out.* Grace decided to stay away for now. If luck was on her side, the couple would catch on, show some decorum and make up something. But by the way they looked, she doubted it.

By this time, Adam entered the galley. Charlotte and Rebecca told him about the couple, but he told them he had seen them. He said he saw the couple moving toward the toilets and the woman went into a cubicle. He thought it was strange that the guy wasn't using one of the other cubicles, but he was sidetracked by another passenger. When he turned around only moments later, the guy wasn't there. At that time he thought, *I bet I know what those two are up to.* He told Rebecca he went by the bathroom to try to hear anything, but he couldn't. Rebecca smiled and said she was going back out into the cabin to help Grace. Adam leaned over to Charlotte and said, "If those two are doing what we all think they are, maybe we should try it. We can get in a quickie before lunch. Don't give me that shy, innocent look as if you don't know what I mean. You're not fooling anyone. I've seen the way you keep checking me out. You've been wanting to get with this for a while." And without hesitation he grabbed his crotch, which was showing his desire.

"You're full of shit, Adam! So much for being shy. I could have you up on harassment charges," Charlotte said with a grin. She then added, "If we get these carts ready for lunch, maybe we'll have a few minutes to spare and have that quickie, but please tell me quickies aren't your thing."

"No way! Only when it's needed. I like to take it slow and steady, to get my women all hot and wet before I bring them back down to earth. You look like a screamer," he said with a sly grin.

(16)

HOW A CONVERSATION ENDED UP IN THE TOILET

Grace kept an eye on the conversation between the Greats and the hippy couple. They had been chatting for some time and Norman had also joined in. Maybe it wasn't all bad and the other couple hadn't revealed the true club rules. Thinking all would be okay, she went on to attend to the other passengers needs. She hoped poor, innocent Katherine and Norman Great were not being corrupted by the filthy-minded Owen and Anna.

The conversation between the two couples seemed, from an outsider's view, to be one of laughter and goodwill. Little did anyone know what was not only being said, but also being planned. It was Katherine that was asking most questions initially and then Norman got into the conversation. As Anna and Owen sat down after their return from "the club," Katherine caught Anna's eye and said she had overheard them talking about seeing if the club was open and she wondered whether Anna would explain what the club was about and if she and her husband could join.

Anna, without any hint of embarrassment or need to lie, replied, "The club? Oh, it's a little thing Owen and I try to do each time we fly. It's not an official club and I hope you won't be offended by what I tell you, but it involves having sex on board the plane, usually in the bathroom, which is why it's called the mile-high club. You're having sex a mile high. Lots of people do it."

"Oh my. This is my husband, Norman." Katherine shook Norman's arm and introduced him to Anna, who likewise introduced both herself and Owen.

"Norman, listen to this. Anna was just telling me about the club I overheard them talking about. It involves having sex on the plane," she whispered.

"Really?" Norman said, now leaning over to hear more.

"Owen and I have been doing it for a while now and trying different things. If you don't want to do the bathroom thing, then try using your hands under a blanket, but you need a good poker face when you are doing that. That can be fun, but we have found that's best left for an overnight flight, when the plane is darker and quieter. You guys should go and have a try, if you want to. It's a lot of fun, but a few things to remember. There's not a lot of room in those toilets and you need to be quick about it. Try to pick a time when basically everyone is seated, like during the movie or when a meal is being served. And you need to be discrete about it, otherwise everyone will know what you've been doing—unless of course that's your thing." She winked. "As this will be your first time, do something basic to start with. Then if you enjoy it, get more adventurous."

"I don't know . . . Norman, what do you think? Do you want to try?" Katherine said with a little too much excitement.

"Well, I am feeling horny thanks to the plane's vibrations," he said. However, Norman, being the man he was, needed to know more and asked, "What do you guys do in there? Do you go all the way, or what?"

"Seeing you haven't done this before and with the lack of room, maybe you should start with a bit of oral sex. Or if you can get your positions right, you'll be able to get a quick fuck in," Owen told them. He looked behind them and said, "Now is a good time, if you want to have a go. Once you get down there, look around and if the coast is clear, go in together. Otherwise one of you go in and the other wait until it's clear, then knock on the door and go in."

Katherine was up and on her way; Norman followed her. Owen noticed they were both able to get into the bathroom at once. Norman gave him a sly thumbs-up as he entered.

"Wow. Who knew they'd be into it? They both seem so shy and quiet, almost churchlike," Anna said to Owen.

"Yeah, I know. I guess you really can't judge a book by its cover."

After ten minutes went by, the Greats were still not back. It took a few more minutes before they returned, looking slightly flushed but very happy.

"Well, what did you think? Are you guys members of the club?" Anna asked.

"I guess we are," Katherine replied, grinning.

"Were you able to get each other off, or what?" Owen asked.

"Well, at first we didn't know who should stand where, so Norman sat on the seat while I gave him a blow job. That got him going, so he told me to kneel on the seat and he entered me from behind." She then whispered into Anna's ear, "I had an orgasm then and there. It was all I could do not to scream out. As you said, we tried to be as discrete and as fast as possible, so it became a bit awkward, but the end result was well worth it."

Anna repeated to Owen what Katherine had just told her. Owen gave a thumbs-up and a sly wink.

"Norman and I left together. The hardest part was opening the door. We had no idea if anyone was waiting outside to use the bathroom. Thank you so much for telling us about it."

"The trick about leaving is to use your best poker face and not look anyone in the eye, if someone is waiting. Or just say the other person needed some help or something like that. Anyway, who really gives a rat's ass?" Owen said.

Katherine said, "You seem to be both very comfortable with yourselves to discuss something like that. I think it's great—we don't meet many people as open as you are."

"No problem. We don't bother with stuff like that. You asked, so we told. Besides, you seem like nice people and you would have been either shocked or interested. I'm glad you were the latter. It's great that you had a good first experience," Owen said.

"Norman and I do like to experiment with different places and we both enjoy the thrill of it all—you know, possibly being caught and all that. I hope I'm not sounding like some sort of weirdo," Katherine said shyly.

"Of course not. Look at us: we love to have sex whenever, wherever; nothing weird about that. One more thing. Once you get comfortable with it and you've tried it a few times, you'll get to know who is a 'club member' on board and sometimes you can swap partners. That makes it a whole lot of fun. You become the teacher and the student all at once." Owen winked at Norman and Katherine.

"How can you tell who likes to do it?" Norman clearly wanted to know.

"It's just a look you get from other passengers, sometimes on board—or in the case of our last trip, we met a couple in the boarding lounge. If you suspect someone may be into it, strike up a conversation and you will soon know. If you use the words 'the club,' such as 'I hope the club is open on this flight,' most will respond. If they don't know what you mean by the club, then you can say you have been on flights where they had a games club or something. They won't be any wiser."

"Thank you so much. Norman and I are always looking for new adventures," Katherine said.

The conversation had been quite casual in tone, even though the subject matter was not for everyone's ears. It soon calmed down to a more basic topic concerning where everyone was going and for what reason; no need to talk in low voices or whispers any longer. At that moment, Grace came by to see if everything was okay and noticed the grins on both Norman and Katherine. She then saw Owen and Anna had similar grins. Grace had an uneasy feeling about the looks she just noticed. *Surely not those two . . . ?* she thought. *They are too innocent looking to be into anything like that.* She left with a horrible thought that the Greats may have been initiated into the club.

(17)

BUSINESS AS NOT-SO-USUAL

So far everything was running smoothly in business class. That was about to change. James had to deal with a passenger who was not feeling very well. James sought out Jen and asked if the passenger could be taken to lie down in one of the first-class seats, which fold down into a bed for longer flights. Jen inquired who the passenger was and then told James she would go and arrange someplace more comfortable. James told her the passenger was Mr. Jonathon Weaver.

"He looked kind of green around the gills when he boarded, but he seemed okay. He said he has some stomach pains and a headache," James told her.

"Could be the flu, or maybe he had some bad food. I'll go and make some space for him and organize some medication," Jen said.

Jen then left to prepare a space for Jonathon to rest in. James told Jonathon that they were going to move him to a more comfortable seat and it would be a few minutes. He was taken to lie down in a reclining seat at the rear of first class, away from the other passengers. Jen gave him a couple of Advil and some Mylanta, to try to help him and she noticed that even in the short time it took to bring him up, he looked worse than before and now turned from green to gray. She gave him some throw-up bags in case he needed them and then left him to rest. She advised Peter and Orla that he was there, but if he looked quiet, not to disturb him. If they thought he was getting worse, they should find her and she would let the captain know. Jen said she would check the passenger manifest to see if there was a doctor on board who may be able to assist if Jonathon became worse. Not finding one, she went back to where Jonathon was resting to find Peter helping him up.

Looking extremely ill, Peter escorted Jonathon to the bathroom and waited outside to offer any assistance. Jen asked Peter if he knew what was bothering Mr. Weaver.

"He is still having stomach troubles, but his headache seems to be clearing. I wonder if it's his appendix or something," Peter told her.

"I'm no doctor, but the fact he needs the bathroom may be a good sign," Jen replied.

"I tried to get any information out of him about what he ate prior to the flight. He said he ate some sushi at the airport but didn't think anything of it. He said it tasted just fine, but who knows with that stuff. I have taken him to use one of the forward toilet cubicles, out of sight of the passengers. I'll wait with him to see if he's okay or needs any assistance. I've told Orla and she said she'd handle the other passengers while I tend to Mr. Weaver."

"I'll stay in first class and help out. You stay with Mr. Weaver until he's more settled. Don't worry about the other passengers," Jen said.

Jen went to help in the cabin. After a few minutes passed, the bathroom door opened slightly. A very pale Jonathon appeared through the gap. He had to explain to Peter that whatever was bothering his stomach had made itself known in a very unfortunate way. "I'm so sorry to ask—believe me, you can't know how embarrassing this is—but do you have any spare trousers on board? Unfortunately, whatever I ate wanted out and it exited at both ends. I cannot believe this is happening. I am so, so sorry to do this to you, but if anything is at all positive about this, I am feeling a whole lot better," Jonathon explained, although he still looked like death warmed over.

"Don't worry, I'll take care of everything. What size are you? Actually, you look to be about the same size as me. I have a spare uniform in my locker in case of an emergency and it looks like this could qualify for one. Lock the door and I'll go and get it. I take it you will need underwear as well? I'll bring a plastic bag and something more substantial than toilet paper to clean yourself up. You can place your stuff in the bag and we can deal with it when we land. I'll be right back and don't worry, nobody will know. Believe me, you're not the first person to go through something like this," Peter said. Discretion was something for which Peter was well-known.

Peter found his spare uniform trousers along with a pair of Calvin Klein briefs he always had in his bag. He was always organized for whatever situation arose. He also did the same for James, who wasn't anywhere close to being organized. He returned via the galley, where he picked up a black garbage bag and found two towels, one which he moistened and the other he kept dry.

When he arrived back, he gently knocked and Jonathon opened the door slightly. Peter handed him the bag and told Jonathon to place his soiled garments in it and tie it up. Moments later Peter passed Jonathon both towels along with the clean trousers and underwear. "You are so kind and again, I'm so sorry I've had to put you through this," Jonathon said.

"Think nothing of it. All in a day's work, as far as I am concerned. I'm just glad you are feeling better. I'll wait outside while you clean up," Peter told him.

It took about ten minutes before Jonathon appeared, looking pale but in less distress. Peter's trousers fit him perfectly. He carried the garbage bag, tied up with his soiled garments and towels and once again Peter took charge by taking the bag from Jonathon. He asked Jonathon if he wanted his garments, or whether the bag should be thrown away.

"If it's okay with you, those pants were kind of expensive, so I'd like to take them and have them cleaned."

"Not a problem. I'll take the bag and place it in a storage closet; you can pick it up when we land," Peter explained.

"You are the most helpful person I have ever met. I would really like to do something for you, so if you don't mind, could I get your name and possibly some contact details, so I can return your clothes to you? I cannot thank you enough for being so understanding."

"Oh please, no need to thank me and no need to do anything for me. As I said, it's all in a day's work. We are trained for all of this stuff. I'm just glad you are feeling better. We can worry about my things later, but you need to rest. I'll help you back to your seat and if you need anything at all, let me or Orla know."

Peter then escorted Jonathon back into the first-class cabin and made sure he was comfortable. He noted Jonathon was soon fast asleep. *Thank goodness that didn't turn out to be worse than it was. The last thing anyone needed was some sort of drama,* he thought.

(18)

A MEETING OF TWO MINDS

Back in economy, the drink carts had been replenished and placed in their cradles, ready for the lunch service, which would begin in about thirty minutes. They were about three hours into the flight, so Grace and Rebecca were in the galley preparing the lunch carts, making sure they had equal numbers of each dish. Economy passengers had a choice of roast beef, chicken stew, or vegetable lasagna. Unlike first class or business class, economy meals came prepared in a plastic tray that had little compartments built in, like a TV dinner. A small bread roll and pat of butter was also supplied separately.

The flight attendants would come by and ask each passenger what their choice of meal and drink would be, but if anything ran out, too bad. They would start at the front of economy and work their way back. One thing the flight attendants did not like was a passenger leaving their seats to use the bathroom while the carts were in the aisle. It meant unlocking the brakes on the cart and heading back up the aisle to clear a path for the passenger to return his or her seat. They always acted as if it wasn't a bother, but it was something they hated.

Charlotte and Adam were tending to passengers. Charlotte made sure she stayed close to Adam so that he did not forget their bathroom date. She wasn't holding anything back with her flirting—something both Thelma and Millicent had noticed.

"That girl is wantin' bad for that boy. She don't hold nothin' back. She reminds me of me when I was courtin' the boys," Thelma said.

"What-choo talkin' about, remind you of you? For one thing, that girl has half the ass you did and she goin' to get further than you ever did," Millie cracked back.

"No you di'in't, girl! You know I was the one those boys always wanted," Thelma proclaimed.

"You crazy. All I remember is you telling me you was goin' street to street like you was entertainin' the troops," Millie scolded.

"Entertainin' the troops? I ain't no Bob Hope! Now, you hush yourself up," protested Thelma. Again the surrounding passengers were laughing, but they were right about Charlotte. She definitely had Adam in her sights and her finger was ready to fire his gun.

She was following him around and trying to find out what they might get up to after they land. When they were near the galley, he said with whisper and a grin, "A drink or two to start, maybe a meal and then who knows? Maybe we'll make our own fun."

"I can't wait!" Charlotte responded.

"Baby, I don't let my women wait for anything," he said.

"You are a piece of work, with this quiet, shy boy routine you have in front of others. But now I'm seeing another side—one I like. I'm gonna get to know who the real Adam is and honey, I will not be showin' mercy," Charlotte replied.

"Well, all I can say is, mercy me," he said, grinning. "I won't be like one of your normal hook-ups, Miss Charlotte. I know all about your escapades. You, my girl, are an open book and I intend on opening you up and reading every page."

Charlotte had a reputation for hooking up if she had an overnight stay someplace. One rumor was she once picked up a male passenger in New York who turned out to be a well-known Yankees pitcher. She had no idea; sports were not one of her interests. They made the tabloids, but she denied it, saying she was just in the picture and not with the guy.

At that point Adam decided to change from Mr. Horny back to Mr. Steward—something that Charlotte found strange, but she thought it was simply another side of Adam. Before they entered the galley, he took a quick look back out in the cabin and said, "Looks like nobody else needs anything out there, Let's help with the lunch carts."

"Yeah, hopefully they'll have everything ready. I hate doing the lunch service. Complaints, complaints, complaints—that's all I hear, especially if we run out of something. Oh well, best get it over with," Charlotte said.

Adam and Charlotte were both snickering at each other when they returned to the galley to help Rebecca and Grace.

"Well, well, well, what have we here? Do we have a romance building between you two?" Rebecca inquired with a snide tone. "Adam, you're blushing. What have you two been doing out there?"

"Nothing!" he said way too quickly, adding to the faux shameful look he was getting from Rebecca. Meanwhile, Grace had taken Charlotte aside and asked if she had behaved with Adam.

"All I can say is, I know a bit more about our shy, quiet Adam—more than you want to know. My behaving in front of Adam may get to a whole new level tonight." She smiled a sly smile.

"Oh god, I hope you remember you have to work with him in the future," Grace warned.

"Oh, I know and I intend on working with him all night tonight. Don't you worry, that boy has got my motor revving," Charlotte said.

In business class, James and Bryson already had their carts ready for lunch and were tending to some passenger requests: a pillow here, some water there. Because they were short staffed, Jen was helping them but had left briefly to see how the others were doing. She returned from first class and said, "My god, that woman is horrid. I have no idea how her staff works for her. She is pure evil. Venom is like water compared to what she sprays everywhere as soon as she opens that foul mouth."

"Let me guess: Miss Wynonna Bertrand the queen bitch of Hollywood, strikes again by the sounds of your tone?" James lamented. "Not fair—I want to see her go off her tits at someone. Can I go up and poke her with a stick, to get her riled up?"

"You cannot! Ms. Diva has requested, in the only way she can, to be left in peace and that 'her area'—can you believe she calls it that?—be curtained off. God, I would like to smack the rich right off her. Who the fuck does she think she is?" Jen said.

Bryson said with surprise, "Jen! I don't think I have ever heard you swear before. Miss Thing up front hasn't gotten to our leader, has she?"

"No, I was every bit the professional with her. I'm just venting because if I have to deal with that again, I need to let some steam out. Now, are you guys ready?" Jen asked.

They were and they started serving.

(19)

ATTENTION ALL PASSENGERS

"Girl, I can see by the look in your eye you are after that handsome white boy, ain't you?" Thelma spoke to Charlotte, albeit quietly.

In a whisper, Charlotte replied, "You know it. I plan to get that man no matter what it takes."

"You go get him, girl! He is one fine three-course meal—I can see that myself! And by the looks of the pants, he is packin' meat," Thelma said.

"Yes, ma'am, he is. If I can help it, I'll be having seconds on all three courses."

"Ooo, go get some, girl!" Thelma said with a laugh.

Charlotte had made her way to the galley after serving Millie and Thelma a drink. She found Adam restocking a cart and preparing the galley for lunch.

Adam said, "Hey, sweet stuff. I had a thought: maybe we should forget that quickie in the bathroom and concentrate on tonight. What do you think?"

"Sounds like a plan. Besides, the natives are getting restless out there, so we may not get a chance anyway. But I have some ideas for tonight," Charlotte replied.

"Oh, I have ideas as well. But first I have to know, are you up for some filthy times, or is your reputation just a myth?"

"You know I am. What did you have in mind?" Charlotte responded as she got closer. Charlotte knew they were safe because she saw Rebecca and Grace attending to some older folks at the front. She was right next to Adam, who, after a quick look behind him, grabbed her and laid a kiss on her lips, causing her to lose balance. She placed her hand behind her to stop herself from falling backward, not realizing she had pressed the PA system's on button.

Unfortunately for Charlotte and Adam, the following conversation was broadcasted through the entire aircraft.

"I think I'll start with these tits of yours and work these nipples, so they are hard enough to cut glass," he said, fondling her breasts. "Then I'd like to get between those thighs of yours and take you to heaven. By the time I'm done with you, there won't be a soul within four blocks who doesn't know what we are up to. I will make sure you are satisfied for a very long time and I do mean *very* long. Do you have any plans for this?" Adam then took Charlotte's hand and placed it on his crotch, where she found out she could put one of those rumors about him to bed.

"Oh my god! Adam, you are huge! I can't wait. I've got to see that thing now!" Charlotte said with a seductive growl.

Adam had the same idea and was still pawing her ample bosom when Rebecca and Grace came rushing in, followed seconds later by Jen.

Adam and Charlotte quickly pulled apart and attempted to make as if nothing was happening—until Jen, after she turned off the PA system, told them everything they had just said was heard by the entire aircraft.

Charlotte was horrified, but Adam didn't seem to care all that much; in fact, he had a huge grin on his face. But both knew they were in big trouble. They also knew they had to face all those passengers out there, who knew what they were up to. Jen told them to get themselves together and she would speak with the both of them after the flight. At that moment, the intercom buzzed and Jen picked up. It was Captain Billy asking what the hell that was all about. She told him she was dealing with it and would let him know the outcome. Captain Billy said he wanted to be with her when she spoke to Charlotte and Adam and that they had better have a good explanation, although he could not think of what their excuse could possibly be.

Out in the cabin area, the passengers' reactions were mixed. Some thought it was the best thing they had ever heard, with comments like, "Good for them—at least somebody's gettin' lucky." The best comment of them all came from Millie and Thelma: "Ooo, that girl gonna have to hold on, cause that boy gonna ride her like she the last call at Disneyland! By the sounds of it, she ain't gonna be walking to walk tomorrow. Her easy bake oven gonna be full of his dough"

Owen leaned over and said to Norman and Katherine, "Sounds like we have two new members who want to join the club."

On the other hand, some passengers were horrified at what they had just heard. "Good god, can you believe we had to hear that trash? Those two need to be fired as soon as possible," one woman said. "I'm going to be lodging a complaint, that's for sure."

All in all, the majority of passengers thought it was just a bit of bad luck and thought it humorous, albeit maybe not for Adam and Charlotte.

Jen grabbed the PA system, turned it on, and said, "Ladies and gentlemen, on behalf of Trans County Airways and the team, we would like to apologize for the indiscretion of two of our crew. Trans County Airways prides itself on providing a professional service and expects our staff to perform to those standards. Once again, please accept our apologies."

After Jen had left the galley, Rebecca and Grace attempted to console a humiliated Charlotte. "There's nothing you can do about it now. What you have to do is go out there and be as professional as you can be. Besides, not everyone knows whose voice that was. It could have been any of us," Rebecca told her.

"I can't face those people now—I'll be a laughingstock. Those two ladies will be especially bad. They have already had some fun with me about Adam," Charlotte said.

This time Grace spoke to her. "I knew you were heading for trouble, but unfortunately you have to go out there and do as good a job as you can do. You'll have to suck it up and take whatever comes your way. At least the two of you didn't swear or say anything too sleazy. If you want, we can talk tonight."

Turning a complete 180 degrees from where she was emotionally, Charlotte said, "I'm not backing out now." She looked to Adam and said, "Adam, we're still on, right?"

Adam replied with a sly grin, looking down at his crotch. "You know I'm still ready."

(20)

COME AND GET IT!

Peter and Orla were just about to start serving lunch in the first-class cabin. They had already asked everyone what their preferences would be and made sure they were ready. Peter heard a strange noise behind him and turned to find James trying to get his attention from the partition between first business.

"Oh my god, did you hear that trash on the PA? Straighties are so gross. It sounded like something you'd hear on the Animal Planet. But how fucking hot was it? That Adam must be enormous if Charlotte the harlot thinks he's big. Wish I could get a sneaky peak. But on to the next subject. How is Bitchy McBitch? I heard she's had a meltdown already. Who'd she pay out on? Did she slap anyone?" James asked.

Peter replied "Just a minor eruption, something about being left alone. Orla is asking her assistants if the queen wants any lunch served. She dare not ask her herself. Is everything okay with you guys?"

"Boring! There has to be more than that. If I do not get a meltdown bulletin, then I will create one myself. It's not every day you get the chance to see Ms. Wynonna Bertrand, the absolute bitch to end all bitches, the queen of mean, the cun—"

"All right, all right, enough of that," Peter interrupted.

James continued with a faux shamed look. "Anyway, all's well back here. Nobody's been a pain so far except for the green Mr. Weaver, poor guy. How is he doing, by the way? Is he okay?"

"He's doing better, but there is something I've got to tell you. I let Jonathon get into my pants," Peter said with a sly grin.

James's eyes almost popped out of his head when he heard this and for the first time he was speechless. He looked as if he was going to faint, so Peter had to quickly tell him the whole story. "Oh god, honey I was just kidding. Fuck, if looks could kill. Anyway he had a moment and needed some trousers, so I lent him my spare uniform. Oh, you poor thing, look at that face! I am so sorry." He added, "What do you think about getting together with Craig and his boyfriend tonight? I haven't asked him yet, because I wanted to get your opinion."

After coming back down to earth, James replied, "Sounds like fun. See if he's interested. Maybe he can recommend a place." He then proceeded to give Peter a smack on the arm.

"Okay, I'll see what he thinks. See you later, sweetness," Peter cooed and as he gave James a quick peck on the cheek.

Orla was in the first-class galley getting her first lunch order ready. She had asked Wynonna's assistants if she desired any lunch but was told not to bother; the diva would bellow if she wanted anything, they told her. Beth and Michele gave Orla their choices and she told them she'd be right back.

Peter was preparing Craig's soup and placed the bowl on a silver tray along with a napkin, in which the cutlery was wrapped. A silver salt-and-pepper shaker set was also provided, beside that sat a crystal wineglass of Chardonnay with a similar crystal glass of ice water. He then placed a crisp white folded napkin over his left forearm, picked up the tray and proceeded to Craig's seat.

In his best hoity-toity voice, he said, "Your soup, sir. I do hope it pleases you."

Craig laughed and in an equally silly voice said, "Why thank you, good sir."

Peter then returned to start another tray. This time he delivered a tray to Paul, set up with a salad he ordered, but he didn't use a silly voice when he served him. He told Paul his steak would be right up and left to serve some other passengers. It wasn't long before Peter returned and removed both Craig's and Paul's first-course trays. He then delivered Craig his chicken dish and Paul's steak. Paul had ordered a beer, which was also on the tray, along with a glass of ice water and napkin-wrapped cutlery. Peter then continued with his other passengers.

While Peter was attending the other passengers, Paul unwrapped the cutlery and swapped the knife with a spoon he'd stashed next to him from the earlier snack service. He didn't think anyone would notice the spoon missing from his snack tray and if anyone asked, he would just shrug his shoulders and say he had no idea. As he thought, Peter didn't even raise an eyelid when removed the tray. During the flight, Paul began to think he may be able to take out his revenge on his mother right here on the plane. He noticed during an earlier bathroom visit that the entrance to Wynonna's enclosed area was not visible by any other person. Sensing an opportunity may present itself, he started to plan his moves. If he could time it just right, he could carry out his attack and nobody would know. This seemed to working out better than Paul had thought. He had never planned on committing the murder on the plane, but the circumstances were falling into place.

Peter noticed Paul signaling him while he was serving another passenger. He walked over to see what Paul needed. Paul told him he didn't get a knife with his cutlery; the new napkin only had a fork and a spoon, but no knife.

"I'm so sorry. I'll bring you a knife right away, Mr. Danielson," Peter said.

"No problem and stop with the Mr. Danielson stuff. Call me Paul," he replied.

Peter returned to the galley to find Orla, who was preparing her next tray. "Our hunk couldn't be more pleasant," Peter told her. "His cutlery had a spoon instead of a knife in it. I'm sure I checked it before I put it on the tray. I'll just grab a knife and run it out to him. He didn't seem upset about it—*and* he told me to call him Paul. Jealous?"

"I wish I was serving him, but I'd be afraid I'd disgrace myself by staring at him. He *is* a dish, isn't he? My lot are okay but dull as dishwater, which is fine with me. Nobody is too demanding so far, except for you know who. I can handle her as long as the others behave themselves. The Wicked Witch of the West has been quiet for some time, maybe she's asleep. God, I hope so," Orla told Peter. They both returned to the cabin.

"Here is your knife, Mr. Danie—sorry, Paul. Please accept my apologies," Peter said.

"Thanks," Paul replied and he began his lunch.

Peter asked Craig if everything was okay. Craig nodded that everything was.

A similar story was unfolding in both business and economy class. So far everyone was happy enough, except Millie and Thelma. Charlotte was dealing with what the two women called a "petite portion problem." Both were entertaining the surround passengers with a pre-lunch show.

"Will you look at the size of this dish? This wouldn't feed an ant. They expect me to be satisfied with this little bundle of nothin'?" Millie got Charlotte's attention. "Looky here, girl. You got anything else back there? 'Cause this here ain't goin' to make a dent. I need some food, girl, not just a sampler pack! I get more food eatin' the samples at Costco."

"That is the lunch size, but let me go back and see if there is anything else left. It may be just another serving. Will that be okay with you?" Charlotte asked.

"Girl, anything you got, I'll take. And don't be forgettin' Miss Thelma, 'cause she be lookin' at me like I'm some fried chicken or somethin'!"

"Okay, let me go and see what we have. I'll be right back," Charlotte said, half laughing.

"Thank you, honey," both Millie and Thelma said. Then Thelma said, "How they expect someone to survive on this little piddlin' amount? You goin' to eat that bread roll?"

"Don't you be eyein' that bread now! I'll slap the black right off that hand, if you go anywhere near it," Millie scolded.

"I was just askin'. Don't be all in my face 'cause you ain't full enough! It's just sittin' there lookin' all sad. What you waitin' for, anyway? Someone to butter it for ya, like you the queen of England or somethin'? Now, where is that girl? I'm starved!" Thelma replied.

(21)

WYNONNA HAS SPOKEN!

The calm in first class was broken when Wynonna made an appearance from behind her curtained compound. "Are either of you going to get me something to eat, or are you just going to sit there wasting away, like you always do!" she bellowed loud enough so the entire cabin had her attention. She was good at that.

"I'll arrange for some food to be sent to you, Ms. Bertrand," Michele said.

"Are you stupid? Get me a menu—I will decide what I want. And you had better make sure they have it. I'm going to the bathroom now and if that menu isn't on my seat when I return, there will be hell to pay!" While departing to use the bathroom, everyone could hear her say, "A fucking waste of time, the both of them."

When Wynonna was behind closed doors, there was a rumbling of conversations among the other passengers. "My god, who does she think she is?" "There would be no way I'd stand for that." "Those poor girls, having to listen to that all day." Paul looked over toward Craig and said, "Is that Wynonna Bertrand? She has some mouth on her, doesn't she?"

Craig replied, "She certainly does and I have firsthand experience with it. I had to work with her on a movie she did with my boss and it was the worst three months I have ever spent with anyone. The old crow even wanted a butler in her trailer while we were on location. Can you believe that? She's like that to everyone, unless she wants something and then she can be a sweet as can be. However, that is a very rare occurrence. I hate the old crone and wish someone would end all our suffering and take a knife to that throat. Hopefully we won't have to hear too much from her. Most likely she will do her usual excessive drinking, which always leads to her being out to it."

"What do you do, may I ask? Are you a director or something?" Paul said.

"I'm Jacob Danulle's assistant. She was working on one of his movies and gave him and everyone else, absolute hell. He won't ever work with her again, no matter how big her star is. I'm Craig Lewis." Craig offered his hand.

"Paul Danielson."

"Are you on vacation, or do you live in California?" Craig asked.

"No, I live in New York. I have a family thing I need to attend. I'll see my mother and be the good son and then the rest of my time will be my own, so I'll take some time to relax and do a bit of sightseeing," Paul said.

"Can I ask what business you are in?"

"I'm in retail—the menswear manager at Barney's New York."

"I see. Have you ever thought about being in a movie? If I can be up front, you have the looks and my boss is always looking for new people. Fact is you have a very familiar face. It's almost like I've seen you on the big screen before. There's no pressure; I can give you my card and if you are interested, give me a call. I can set something up for you, maybe while you're in town."

"I don't know. I've never done any acting. My roommate is an actor, though. Can I think about it?" he said, reaching for Craig's card.

"As I said, no pressure. Let your roommate know as well, if you want. My boss isn't anything like that bitch." Craig pointed toward the front of the plane at Wynonna emerging from the bathroom.

Paul thought to himself, *If you only knew why my face is so familiar. Part of* Mommy Dearest *will at least live on.*

Waiting just outside of Wynonna's section was Michele, Beth and Orla. "Get me a Scotch straight up. I'll have the chicken," Wynonna said as the menu came flying out from behind the curtains.

"Right away, Ms. Bertrand," Beth said.

Beth and Michele followed Orla to the galley. They all wanted to make sure everything was right.

"Both you girls are saints. There is no way I could do it, that I can tell you. I'd have to silence that trap for good," Orla said.

"Not to worry. This will be the last time she gets to treat us like crap. After this flight, she will no longer have us to talk down to and she'll pay, don't worry about that," Beth said.

Orla gave Beth the drink and told Michele to wait while she got Wynonna's meal ready. She didn't think too much about what the girls had just said. Orla had had to deal with some ornery passengers, before but none like Wynonna Bertrand.

(22)

THE CLEANUP

All three cabins were now clearing up after the lunch service and all that remained, apart from the occasional request, was a second drink service later in the flight. The usual post-lunch bathroom lines were forming, which gave the flight attendants time to tidy up and sort the cabin out.

In business class Bryson and James were just about finished. James told Bryson he'd be back in about fifteen minutes; he said he wanted to catch up with an old friend seated in first class. Bryson didn't mind because Jen was around somewhere. James then made his way up to pay a visit to Craig, who he found having a chat with the hunk next to him, so James thought this would be good time to be introduced.

"Hey Craig, thought I'd come up and have a quick chat. Oh sorry, didn't mean to interrupt."

"Hi, James. This is Paul Danielson. I'm trying to convince him to see Jacob while he is in town. Don't you think he has the star look?" Craig asked.

"He sure does. Hi, I'm James. Nice to meet you."

"Nice to meet you, James. I'll let you guys continue with your chat. Craig, I'll let you know about seeing Jacob." Paul then stood up and stretched his legs. He was on another recognizance mission. More and more he felt the time was close to saying good-bye to Mommy.

"Oh my god, that guy is one hunk-o-rama, if I ever did see one. Peter and I saw him in the boarding lounge before the flight," James said.

"Me too. He sure does have a look. Jacob would love to see him in front of a camera," Craig replied.

"How about that intercom interlude earlier? What a pair of sluts. God knows what those breeders get up to. The whole thing's a horror. Hot though, wasn't it?"

"Well, it was an eye—or, should I say, ear-opener, I'll tell you. It would make a great storyline in a book, you know it's going in the vault to tell Jacob at a later time. He'll use it somewhere," Craig said with a laugh.

Both left the subject of Adam and Charlotte, chatting more about school days and what came after. By this stage, Peter had joined them and said Wynonna was out of it. "She's had about six Scotches." James told Craig that if he wasn't busy tonight, the four of them could have dinner somewhere. They decided to give each other their cell phone numbers; Craig had to make sure Patrick had nothing planned. He would call them as soon as he knew. He also asked Peter and James if he should invite Paul along and both thought it was a great idea.

Neither one of them noticed that Paul was in earshot and had heard the news that Wynonna was indeed out for the count.

Not long after, James made his way back to business class to find that Bryson had cleaned up and was sitting back relaxing in the galley. In usual Bryson style, he was singing another Barry White song. Peter went to make sure Jonathon was okay and Craig decided to read the in-flight magazine and probably doze off.

In economy, the cleanup took a lot longer, but all four flight attendants were getting a handle on it with Jen's help.

"Thank goodness we had extra meals on board. Do you know those two ladies up front had three servings each?" Charlotte told Jen and Grace.

"I'd rather get rid of it than throw it out," Jen said.

Grace added, "The Greats were happy with their meal, I must say. They were so nice, saying how much they enjoyed the meal and they couldn't believe they were getting such good food. Can you believe that? They think airline food is gourmet or something. They are so sweet. Now I really want to make up a bag for them with some goodies. Is that okay with you?" she asked Jen.

"Sure, go right ahead. In fact, come with me. I'll open up the gift closet and see what we have. Oh, did you ever get to find out if the other couple told them what the so-called club was about? "Jen replied.

"No and I'm not going to ask. The less I know, the better."

Adam came in and announced the two ladies were at it again.

"I need to get to the bathroom. Could you move your ol' heifer ass out my way?" Millie said.

"Who you callin' a heifer you old mule? Damn, girl, you need to go learn some manners or somethin'. Besides, I got to go too, so hush your mouth and don't do no pushin'." Thelma responded.

"I ain't no bulldozer, which is what I'd need to move that ol' buffalo butt you got," Millie said with a laugh.

"Girl got no manners. Brought up wrong, that's what it is. Downright rude, that's right," Thelma muttered to herself, but she made sure everyone could hear.

After Thelma and Millie left, those passengers seated around them started to have conversations, saying things like, "Those two have made this flight the most enjoyable one I have ever been on," and "Forget the video entertainment—they are the entertainment on this flight!" Even though the bathrooms were about fifteen rows behind them, those seated next to them could still hear the two ladies bickering at one another—and judging by the laughter, the passengers down there were getting a taste as well.

"I told you, don't do no pushin'! It's goin' to take as long as it takes. These others got to go first," Thelma scolded Millie.

"I ain't pushin' nothin'. Just you move your sad self up there," Millie replied.

When they finally made it and were next to use the bathroom, the door opened and a large white woman came out with two kids. Thelma took one look inside and said, "Look at the size of this here john! Who fits in here, a midget? Damn, girl, how you fit in there with them youngin's? They have to be pancakes by now."

It was Millie's turn to use the bathroom opposite Thelma's. This time the door opened and a dreadlocked backpacker came out. A green cloud seemed to follow. "Oh damn, hoo! What y'all been eatin'? Man, that's bad. Turnin' me pale, that is. I'm goin' to end up like Michael Jackson, breathin' in that mess. See a damn doctor or eat some damn fruit. Something's wrong with that boy," she said as she walked in.

Thelma emerged and told the next person in line, "Smallest john I ever did see. You'll be okay—you a skinny little thing. Go ahead, you'll be all right."

When both women had returned to their seats, they started on how small the bathrooms were.

"Girl, you see the size of them johns? How you fit your heifer ass in there?" Millie said, laughing.

"I ain't talkin' to you till you get some manners. And *you're* the one with the ass so big, Paramount use it to show their movies on. It's so big, ya'll need a king-size sheet for your drawers. Now hush yourself; I'm going to sleep a spell," Thelma responded and she quickly made out like she was asleep.

(23)

TRICK OR TREAT

The flight crew had finished their lunch and all was set for the final one and a half hours until they landed in LA. Stu decided this was a good time to stretch his legs, so he left the cockpit and made his way to the first-class galley area. He found Peter tidying up and started a conversation.

"Hey, Pete, how's it going out here?"

"No troubles. Well, we had one small drama with a passenger, which was dealt with and of course Bertrand the bitch has had a few boil-overs, but they were minor. All is quiet at the moment," Peter replied.

"That's good. We only have about ninety minutes to go. Can I run something by you?" Stu asked. Peter told Stu to go ahead and he stopped what he was doing to listen. "You know how I'm dating Max's sister, right?"

Peter did not. In fact, up until this bit of news, he thought Stu was dating Max, but he wanted to know more, so he faked like he did. "Oh yeah. I heard you were dating someone. I didn't realize it was Max's sister," he said.

"Anyway, we've been dating for a while now and it has become really serious. So I decided it was the time to pop the question, which I was going to do tonight, but fuckin' Max has ruined all that by volunteering the both of us to go to a seminar tonight. He *knew*

I was going to propose soon and he knew I was seeing her tonight. Fuck, he pisses me off," Stu said angrily.

"Can't you get out of the seminar?" Peter asked.

"No. Captain Havilland told the both of us we have to attend. If Max hadn't opened his big mouth, then the captain wouldn't have thought it a good idea we attend. I'm really pissed off right now. Anyway, I had better get back in there. Thanks for listening—I just needed to vent," Stu said.

"No problem, anytime," Peter replied.

Stu left to go back to the cockpit and Peter immediately went to find James to tell him everything. He knew James was going to go ballistic with all this new information. Armed with his gossip, Peter found James dealing with a late request from one of his passengers. He waited for him in the galley and before too long James appeared. James had to tell Peter to breathe because he was almost beside himself, trying to get the story out. After hearing all Peter told him, James seemed confused.

"You say Stu is dating Max's sister?" James asked.

"I'm telling you, that's what he told me," Peter replied.

"It doesn't make any sense. Stu is dating Max's sister? Does Max even *have* a sister? We both thought Stu was dating Max. How about that time we heard them talking? Remember, they didn't know we were in the next room and they sounded very intimate. Are you sure that's what he said?"

"Go and ask him yourself, if you don't believe me," said Peter.

"All right, keep your bra on, missy. Who could have come up with this scenario? Now that's a kick to the rubber bits, I must say. Stu and Max's sister? Damn," James replied.

"I know. I would have given those guys a lifetime membership to the Barbra Streisand, Cher, Bette Midler and Lady GaGa fan emporium, the way they carry on. I'm going to ask Orla—she will know what's going on. This cannot be right. We are never wrong and both our gaydars have been going crazy over those two. I'll get back to you when I find out more."

Peter then left to go and find Orla and to get this drama sorted out. Neither he nor James would be able to concentrate on anything until they found out what the true story was. James bumped into Rebecca and could not contain himself. He told her all the new gossip, but he was not to know she was already in on the setup, as were all the other crew. Rebecca did her best not to spill the beans and played her part well. She told James, "That's insane. Stu isn't dating Max's sister—he's already married."

"What! I cannot believe this! First Peter says, per Stu's own words, that Stu is dating Max's sister. Now you say Stu is married? Why have I never heard this before? You have to mistaken," James said. He was so flustered he could barely speak.

"I don't think so. I've seen the wedding photos," Rebecca replied. "I have one way you could find out, though: ask Stu," she continued.

Rebecca returned to economy class trying to contain her laugh. James had the look of someone about to explode with all this gossip. He went to find Peter and to find out what was going on. He didn't get far. He found Grace and asked her if she knew about Stu.

Grace said Stu was married but was now separated. She also heard he was bisexual because he was dating a drag queen. James collapsed into an empty seat—he couldn't take much more. He had to find out what was what. So far, he had heard three different stories. Once he found a bit of composure, he left to seek out Peter. He found him in conversation with Orla in the business-class galley.

"You won't believe what I have heard!" James butted in.

"Wait a minute. Listen to what Orla has just told me," Peter said.

"Stu isn't dating Max's sister. They are already married. They met when Max was involved with Stu's aunt. It turned out Stu's aunt was already married and was having an affair with Max, which didn't turn out well. Stu isn't too popular with his family at the moment, because he is involved with a member of Max's family," Orla explained.

"Then why did he tell Peter he wanted to propose tonight?" James said, even more flustered.

"I don't know. Maybe he didn't want you guys finding out. Who knows?" she said.

"So is Max bisexual or not?"

Murder Midair

"Bisexual? Who told you that?"

"Rebecca told me. She said he was dating this woman who turned out to be a drag queen and was involved with him for some time," James replied.

"Now you say it, I did hear something, but that's not what I remember. I remember Max being propositioned by a lady, but when he realized she was a he, Max was put off and didn't take it any further," Orla said.

"This is insane. We both thought Stu and Max were gay. Then we hear Stu is going to propose to Max's sister—the sister he is supposedly already married to! The sister whose brother did or did not screw around with a drag queen and had an affair with an already married aunt. It's too much! Something is going on."

At that moment, some of the crew had appeared. Max and Stu came over to where Orla, Peter and James were, then right in front of them they French-kissed each other. The crew all started to laugh, including Jen, who had just shown up. It took a while before Peter and James realized they were the butt of a joke and that the entire crew was involved. When they asked why they were being picked on, everyone told them they had it coming; their constant gossiping was becoming way too much, so the crew got together to play this very funny but harmless trick on them. James looked pissed, but Peter saw the funny side. Peter said they were sorry and promised to keep their gossiping in check from now on. James just grunted, but everyone knew this was not going to be the end of it. As the crew members returned to where they were supposed to be, they heard James mutter to Peter, "See? I knew those two were gay. I just *knew* it."

Paul used this opportunity while the crew was busy to make his move. He noticed Craig and the other passengers were sleeping, watching their screens, or reading. He knew the bathroom area was free. He retrieved the knife he had stashed and hid it in his trouser pocket. The time had come. No one saw Paul leave or return to his seat.

(24)

THE DESCENT

Most passengers were having a nap, reading, or utilizing the bathroom to freshen up. The flight had about sixty minutes until they landed. Paul was just sitting down as Peter and Orla returned from all the drama with the crew. Craig was napping with a magazine on his lap. Both Beth and Michele were down toward the rear of the cabin, chatting to one another. Peter noticed they looked to be very secretive and both seemed worried about something. Jonathon was awake but not in any distress; he just sat quietly while the cabin buzzed around him.

Orla asked Paul if he needed anything before they landed. He said he was okay, but she noticed he must have splashed some water in the bathroom because his trousers were wet on the left thigh. His sleeve was also wet. *Those bathroom faucets are touchy sometimes,* she thought. Wynonna hadn't been heard from since she'd finished her lunch and six Scotches. Orla would have to wake her before they landed—something she was dreading. She decided to leave it until the last minute and then run. What did she care, anyway? She was off to Thailand tomorrow and nothing and no one would dampen her spirits.

Back in economy, Thelma woke to find Millie had fallen asleep on her shoulder. The passengers around them were involved in sleeping, reading, or watching the movie, which was just finishing. Thelma decided to freshen up but first had to remove Millie from her shoulder. She decided to be tactful about it so as not to disturb the others around them.

"Millie, honey," she cooed softly. No response.

"Millicent, baby girl," she said slightly louder.

When Millie hadn't responded after about four attempts, Thelma's tact went out the window. "Girl, you better get this ol' bowling ball you call a head off of my shoulder now!" she yelled.

Millie responded with a moan and moved her head. As Thelma went to the bathroom, she heard Millie say, "That girl don't have no manners. I'm gonna have to have a talk with her, teach her some. Mmm hmm, that's what I'm gonna do." Nobody was listening, so she decided it would be best to use the bathroom as well.

Grace had put together two gift bags and presented them to Norman and Katherine. Both were beside themselves with excitement and they could not stop thanking Grace and Jen who had also turned up. They said how much they enjoyed the trip and they had a little giggle to themselves when they said it, both looking at Owen and Anna. They admitted they were a little frightened about the landing. Jen and Grace tried to put them at ease. Grace told Jen she was sure that the hippy pair next to them had corrupted them.

In all the cabins, the crew went through collecting any trash. They were due to land in thirty minutes and the plane was now making the initial descent into LA International. In a few moments, Jen would be making the announcement right after Captain Billy made his.

"Ladies and gentlemen, this is your captain speaking. We are now on our descent into Los Angeles. The local time in LA is 12:50 p.m. and the temperature is seventy-eight degrees with clear, blue skies. We hope you have enjoyed your flight and we hope you have a great time in LA, or if you have a connecting flight, enjoy the rest of your trip."

Jen's voice then came over the PA system. "Ladies and gentlemen. As you just heard, we are now on descent into Los Angeles. We ask you to make sure your tray tables are locked away and your seats placed in the upright positions with your seat belts fastened.

The crew will be making their way throughout the cabin to remove any trash you may have. For those with connecting flights, a Trans County Airways representative will be waiting at the arrival gate to direct you to your next flight. We hope you have enjoyed your flight and we look forward to seeing you on board in the future. Once again, I wish to apologize for the earlier indiscretion by our crew members. Thank you for flying Trans County Airways."

As soon as Jen placed the microphone back in the holder the intercom buzzed, meaning another member of the crew was calling from elsewhere in the plane. It was Orla, sounding quite distressed. She needed Jen in first class immediately.

(25)

DEATH OF A DIVA

Jen arrived to find Orla, Peter, Beth and Michele waiting outside the still-curtained area surrounding Wynonna's seat. Seeing where they were, her first thought was, *Oh what fresh hell am I in for now?* She thought somebody had upset Wynonna and she had gone off about something.

Peter took Jen aside to explain what had happened. Orla was very shaken and needed to regain her composure. Peter said Orla went to let Wynonna know they were starting to land and the curtains needed to be opened. She discovered Wynonna still sleeping with a blanket covering her, or so she thought. Orla was unable to wake her up with the sound of her voice, so she gave Wynonna a shake. At this stage, Orla didn't think too much of it because she knew Wynonna had had at least six or seven Scotches and was probably out of it. It was when Orla gave Wynonna a slight shake that she noticed a strange bump underneath the blanket. Orla started to remove the blanket and found Wynonna had been stabbed through the heart and was dead, the knife still embedded in her. Peter went on to explain how he took Beth and Michele aside and told them what had happened. Nobody else knew what had happened, although some of the passengers had a concerned look on their faces. Jen told Peter to stay with Orla while she called the cockpit to advise the captain.

"Captain, I am very sorry to disturb you while you are busy, but there has been an incident in the first-class cabin involving Wynonna Bertrand," Jen said.

Captain Billy replied, "Oh who upset her this time? We have had a nearly drama-free flight and with twenty minutes to go, somebody made the old bitch go off her head? God, I will be glad to get rid of her and I hope we never have to deal with her again. Tell me what happened."

"Well, it looks like she's been stabbed. She's dead," Jen said bluntly.

"What are you talking about? This is not the time to be making jokes, Jen." Captain Billy sounded annoyed. Thank goodness he had given the landing duties to Stu so he was able to deal with this new drama.

"It's not a joke! Orla found her. We still have her seat curtained off, so none of the other passengers know what has happened—but they do know something is going on."

"Oh my god! Okay, get everyone seated but keep the area curtained off. I'll advise LAX what has happened. Make sure no one departs the aircraft when we get to the gate, although the authorities may hold us away from the gates until they board. I'll advise the passengers as soon as I know what the authorities want us to do. I won't say what the problem is and it's best kept that way until we know more. Try to act as calmly as possible and tell the others to do the same."

As Billy thought, the response from the tower was that the plane would be held while the authorities boarded; the plane would then be towed into the arrival gate. In all his twenty-five years flying commercial aircraft, he had never had a major incident on one of his flights. Now he had a death—a murder no less—and to make matters worse, the person was a huge star. *Thank goodness Jonathon Weaver seems to be okay after his troubles earlier. It's going to be a long day,* he thought. *So much for going to Vermont.*

"Ladies and gentlemen, this is Captain Havilland. We are now on final approach to LA International. We have been advised that we will not be heading directly to our allotted arrival gate because there is a holdup with another aircraft utilizing the space. It should only be a slight delay. We will be held nearby until our allocated space becomes available. Sorry for the inconvenience." This sometimes happened, which was why he told the passengers that. The authorities confirmed they would be held on the tarmac and would be boarded by the LAX airport police. Nobody would be allowed to depart from the aircraft. Once the crime scene was secured, they would be towed to the gate. Captain Billy knew as soon as the passengers saw police vehicles approaching, they would realize something was wrong. He had thought about telling the passengers that they had a sick passenger, using Jonathon as an excuse, but that wouldn't have made any sense because the aircraft wouldn't be stopped from getting to the gate for a sick person—in fact, they would want the aircraft to get to the gate as soon as possible so that they could attend to the passenger quickly. He had to think of something quickly. No matter what, they had to concentrate on landing because they were now on approach and the runway was directly ahead.

(26)

HIDE THE DONUTS—IT'S THE FUZZ

By the time the plane landed, news that something was wrong began to spread throughout. Peter had told James, who, being the bigger of the two gossips, told Charlotte, whose mouth was just a tad too big for her own good and was overheard by some passengers. It was like one of those games kids played at school, where one whispered to another and then passed it on, until the original story became entirely different and much more dramatic.

The story started by Peter telling James, "Wynonna was found dead." It ended up in economy class with a story that Wynonna had killed a flight attendant and had the flight crew bailed up.

One thing was absolutely certain: nobody knew who could have killed Wynonna, because she was curtained off in such a way that unless somebody was walking by, no one could be seen entering or leaving her area. When the aircraft came to a halt on the tarmac, those who had window seats noticed police vehicles approaching, lights ablaze. Now the chat grew louder and people demanded to know what was going on. Of course Millie was in a state and was one of those wanting to know.

"Something big is happening, Thelma! Police are everywhere down there. Looks like an episode of *COPS* or something!"

"Give me a look here, now. You think every time you see a police officer, you gonna be on TV. Well, look at that! Something sure ain't right, whatever it is. I heard LA is a rough town, but this is ridiculous!" Millie started singing the *COPS* tune.

At the moment, Charlotte came by, so Thelma and Millie grabbed her and asked, "What are all those police doing around this plane? I heard some scuttlebutt that Wynonna Bertrand strangled somebody up there in first class. She's a bitch, you know. I heard she told *Entertainment Tonight* to go fuck themselves when they asked her something she didn't wanna hear. That woman is bad!"

Thelma said, "Millie, the mouth on you. Hush yourself and pray God wasn't listenin'."

"Oh, hush your own self. I heard you say worse than that in church and don't be given me that 'holier than thou' look! I heard you and God heard you too," Millie replied.

Charlotte said, "Ladies, I don't have all the details, but I can assure you Wynonna Bertrand did not kill anyone. All I know is something has happened and the police need to board the plane. Once they are aboard, they will allow everyone off as soon as possible. I'm sure it won't be too much longer." She repeated the message to other passengers around them.

"I know that woman's gone crazy or something. The mouth on her! She treats everyone like she owns them. They should lock her up and smash that key up," Thelma said, not listening to whatever Charlotte said.

Millie chimed in and said, "Lord, have mercy on whoever she killed up there. She on her way to hell three times over."

An announcement came over the PA system. "Ladies and gentlemen, my name is Captain Church from the LAPD. There has been an incident on board and an investigation is underway. We will be towed into the arrival gate and we will be allowing you to depart in sections once we have established what has happened. I will make sure you are not kept on board for very long. Those passengers with immediate connections, please make yourself known to a flight attendant so we can get you to your next flight as soon as possible. Please remain seated and a member of the LAPD will come by to talk to you. We thank you for your cooperation."

Ian Church had been a police officer for twenty-five years. He started as a rookie in Eureka, California, until he was promoted through the ranks. Now he headed up the homicide squad in LA. Balding and slightly overweight, he had seen a side of human nature that nobody needed to see. Sometimes he couldn't believe how cruel the human race was to each other. He entered the aircraft through the front door, along with six uniformed police and four plain-clothes detectives. Soon the plane was buzzing with excitement about what actually happened.

(27)

EXIT, STAGE RIGHT!

Once the aircraft was safely at the gate, the police started to let passengers whom they were certain knew nothing depart; down in economy, that was everyone. Three uniformed police were down there, escorting the passengers off.

Lilly Goldsmith did not look the part of an LA policewoman. Although she had the bright blonde hair and white teeth of a proverbial Californian, she looked more at home at the Playboy mansion—in fact, she looked like one of those strippers who wore fake police outfits. However, she was an extremely talented policewoman, someone who had her fellow officers' respect. Her intuition and competence belied her appearance.

Dave Handler equally did not look the part of a police officer. He had jet-black hair worn shoulder length and his uniform did not hide the body of a person who knew his way around a gym. He was incredibly handsome and everyone from the lowest criminals to his superiors commented about his looks. He once posed for a recruiting poster for the LA police department and the applications doubled during that time.

Accompanying them was Steven Hottle. He was obviously the senior member because he was giving out instructions to the others. Steven was thirty-three, had brown hair, stood about five feet eight and had a slight gut. He knew his time as a policeman was coming to an end; he no longer had the urge to do the job. He decided, along with his wife, to try something new. He just didn't know what that would be.

Lilly and Dave stood at the partition between economy class and business class, one on each side. Steven went and spoke to Charlotte, Rebecca, Adam and Grace. He told them he was going to let the passengers depart in groups, starting with the forward five rows. Millie and Thelma were in the first five rows and waited patiently.

One row in front sat Douglas and Gavin, two very obvious gay fellows in their late teens to early twenties. Thelma had noticed them earlier in the flight and nudged Millie to tell her they had some "delicate boys" by them. Millie responded with, "Don't be nasty to them, now. They both just young ones and cute as can be." Throughout the flight, Thelma struck up some small talk with the two boys and soon she found out they were very decent young men. Gavin and Doug both laughed at everything Millie and Thelma said and at one time Doug high-fived Thelma. Both boys seconded the ladies' opinion of Bryson—until Dave stood by them.

"Good god in heaven! Check out Mr. Policeman. Hot damn, he can cuff me anytime," Doug said, much to the delight of Thelma.

"Child, you said it. Mmm, that man can take me downtown whenever he feels like it!"

Gavin chimed in. "He bends my banana." That had all four screaming with laughter.

"Forget bending your banana, baby. He makes my banana peel," said Doug. That was enough for Millie and Thelma, who were laughing so hard that no sound came out. Other passengers around them also had a giggle. Little did anyone know that Dave could hear everything that was being said. He was used to it and had a smile on his face to show his he didn't mind.

"You see Miss Thing over there, with that Hollywood star look she has going?" Gavin said, pointing to where Lilly stood. Both Gavin and Doug were envious of her look, but being two young gay guys, they decided bitchy was the way to go.

"Check her out—she thinks she's Pamela Anderson or something. This ain't *Baywatch,* Miss Thing!" Doug said.

"Yeah, don't think some hunk is gonna jump in and save you," Gavin chimed in. "What does she think this is, Hugh Hefner's private jet?"

Doug made a different, less snide remark by saying she did look great in that uniform and Gavin agreed. "Love her hair." They put the bitchiness away for now.

(28)

IT'S QUESTION TIME

With the help of the cabin crew, Steven, Lilly and Dave started to get passengers off the plane. In business class, a similar situation had already started, but those who traveled in first class were held back for more detailed questioning. Wynonna's area had been kept curtained so as not to upset any passengers. A plain-clothes detective was questioning Beth and Michele. Peter and Orla were standing by the exit, assisting those who had been questioned and were allowed to depart. They both knew they would have to answer the same questions and Peter had become quite nervous. When both economy and business class cabins were cleared of passengers, the remaining crew was told to make their way up to first class to be questioned as well.

Craig was next to be questioned and said he didn't see or hear anything, because he was sleeping most of the flight after lunch; Orla and Peter reiterated that fact. He told the police the only people he spoke with were Rebecca, Peter, James and Paul. He was asked to supply some contact details and was free to go, but he was told he would be contacted if they needed anything more from him.

Beth was visibly shaken and was sitting down by herself while Michele was chatting with an officer. Their roles were reversed soon after and Michele was left by herself while Beth was questioned. Michele had a somewhat nonchalant attitude about her, which did not help her. Neither was allowed to leave the aircraft. As Craig departed, he gave Peter his card and told him to call when he and James were allowed to leave; they would meet up later that evening. If Patrick had to work, then the three of them, along with Rebecca and Paul, could go somewhere.

Paul was now being questioned and two officers were with him. They asked him what he was doing in LA, where was he from, what he did for a living—the same questions that were asked to the other people. He was asked to stand aside and not leave for now, because they could have a few more questions for him. For the first time, Paul began to sweat a little.

The last passenger to be questioned was Jonathon. Although he felt a whole lot better, he still was very weak and looked pale, but he answered the questions as best he could. Peter was asked to verify that Jonathon was indeed moved from business to first class because he was ill and that Peter had escorted him to the bathroom.

Soon, all that remained were Paul, Beth, Michele and the crew. An ambulance had been called and the coroner was on his way. Paul was taken aside by another plain-clothes officer and after answering some more questions he was allowed to leave. He gave Peter his cell phone number and asked him to call concerning dinner. Earlier, Peter had mentioned having to provide Paul with a knife because he was missing the one for lunch, which was why the police wanted to question him further. Paul told them a similar story and it seemed legitimate. He said the knife was missing from his lunch order so he asked for another. Peter confirmed this and told the officer he did remove a knife off Paul's tray after lunch, so it wasn't the one used in the killing.

The police were questioning both Beth and Michele, because Orla had said both girls had made remarks earlier concerning getting rid of Wynonna. Both girls said they meant they were going to quit because of her being so mean—they didn't intend to get rid of her by killing her.

When Orla was questioned, she told them she had gone to retrieve Wynonna's lunch tray and at the time Wynonna was asleep.

James Austin

She said she noticed her napkin was thrown to one side but decided to leave it there so as not to disturb Wynonna; she would have had to walk around her to get it. She thought it best to not wake her if she didn't have to. That was the last time she saw her until she went to wake her up.

(29)

THE INVESTIGATION

The police had nobody to pin the crime on and it frustrated Detective Church to no end. All he knew was that someone on board did it. Unable to hold anybody, the police had no option but to let everyone leave. They had all the contact details for all the passengers, so the best thing to do was to allow the forensics team in to see whether they could find any evidence to find the murderer. One area of interest was the forward bathroom. Because Wynonna wanted the area surrounding her seat curtained off, no one could see the bathroom from his or her seat, so anybody could have used it as a place to get rid of any evidence. Along with that, no one could see whether anybody entered Wynonna's area, which made it perfect to carry out the killing. The only thing baffling the detectives was how the killer would know whether the bathroom was or wasn't being used and why was it so clean. They told the forensic team to make sure they covered that area with a fine-tooth comb. Once Wynonna was killed, they would probably want to utilize the bathroom to get rid of any evidence, or maybe they just lucked out or were extremely good at what they did—which sent shivers down the detectives' spines.

Detective Church was trying to think like a killer in order for any of this to make sense. If Wynonna had had too much to drink, she may have been sleeping it off and would not have heard anyone enter. Her assistants said they didn't hear Wynonna talking to anyone except, her rants during the flight. The last time they'd heard anything from her was about thirty minutes after lunch, when she demanded another Scotch; after that she was quiet and they assumed she was sleeping because she always drank too much. None of this was unusual, as far as they were concerned. Neither one was going to risk any more screeching to see if she was okay. They had no reason to think anything was wrong.

After the plane had been emptied of passengers and crew, it was towed to a hanger for the investigation to continue. Wynonna's body was removed via a rear-door lift and was taken to the morgue to be autopsied. By this stage, the press had caught wind, and the Trans County Airways officials were in warp mode trying to get a press release out. This case was quickly reaching a dead-end, with Detective Church and his team at a loss—although not all the Forensic details had come in. With luck, they would find something to give them some direction to follow. Whoever did this was very good at hiding his or her tracks. One question that was constantly crossing Detective Church's mind: Why would anyone want to kill Wynonna Bertrand? The world knew she was a hard woman with an evil temper, but that was no reason to kill her.

Once the plane was in the hanger, the forward bathroom was taken apart and scrutinized thoroughly, along with the seats that had been curtained off. The contents of the holding tank, which contained the toilet waste, had to be cleared out as well—something nobody volunteered for. But being a forensics officer meant anything could be evidence, so everything had to be checked. One thing the investigation did find was evidence that the bathroom had been wiped clean at sometime during the flight. A napkin was also found among the toilet waste, which was a strange thing to find. Analysis found it to be the same type of napkin used during the lunch service in the first-class cabin. Unfortunately, it didn't hold any clues because the chemicals used to treat the toilet waste had rendered any possible evidence useless.

(Paul's Internet research had paid handsomely with this information and he used it well.)

Wynonna's body underwent an autopsy, which revealed she did die from a single stab wound straight through the heart. Being intoxicated didn't help and probably made the situation worse; she probably didn't feel a thing. One thing discovered during the autopsy was that Wynonna's liver wasn't going to survive her drinking. Even more interesting was that she had at one time given birth. That piece of information had not been known to anyone and was cleverly kept quiet for decades. It was now out there for all to know, because the autopsy results would become public fodder as soon as they were released. *The press is going to have field day with this,* Detective Church thought.

Some of the headlines to appear in the days after the autopsy results were made to entice the public to read: "Wynonna Bertrand Death: Hollywood Diva's Destiny's (Love) Child." Another less polite rag's headline read, "Diva Death Reveals Brawl over Baby Bundle: Wynonna Bertrand's Long Lost Child Appears out of Nowhere to Claim the Fortune."

The best headline was, "Yenta Wynonna, Death Becomes Her! Wynonna Bertrand's Jewish Roots Revealed and Her Forgotten Child Found on the Streets."

The reporters with these lowlife papers had absolutely no credibility and if they couldn't find the truth, they would make something up. Sometimes they would ignore the truth if it wasn't as juicy as their made-up story. They paid a street person to pretend to be Wynonna's abandoned child. Nobody knew who or where this person was. As they aid, money changed everything.

Once the legitimate press had revealed the situation with Wynonna's child, they made it known they would pay handsomely for anyone who would come forward with information. Her death took second fiddle to this spicy bit of gossip.

It didn't take long before a woman in Nevada came forward. She said she was once a midwife who had helped a young woman named Wynonna Strausman, about twenty-five years ago. She said the girl was about eighteen and fell pregnant while dating some Hollywood star. "I remember her saying she didn't want the child, but she was too far gone to have an abortion. She asked me to adopt it out—she wanted nothing to do with it. She didn't even want to know if was a boy or a girl. Turns out it was a boy. She gave birth and the next day she was gone."

Francine Woods had been a midwife for ten years when she met Wynonna. She had plenty of work in Nevada, because at that time it was the only state with legal brothels, which were a refuge for unmarried, pregnant girls so that they would take them in and give the girls shelter. She opened up to the tabloids and they paid her well for her story. One thing the paper couldn't work out was how the tabloid rag knew about Wynonna's Jewish past; they just put it down to some fluke guesswork to make sales.

Francine said, "One day this teenage girl showed up asking for an abortion. Even then, she was a foul-tempered thing, demanding this and that. She screamed the place down when I told her she waited too long to have an abortion and she'd have to carry to full term. Once she realized this, she decided to stay on. But once she gave birth, I never saw her again—until I heard the name Wynonna, when she started to become famous. I always wondered if it was the same girl because it's not a common name. I think I may know who the father is as well, but that will cost you more." Francine was no idiot.

The tabloids were going nuts with this stuff. Not only did Wynonna Bertrand, the queen bitch of Hollywood, have a child, but she was once Wynonna Strausman—she was born Jewish! After the dollars were increased, they asked who Francine thought the father was and she said all she remembered was the name Bruce. "Wynonna kept saying the name Bruce while she was with us."

The papers quickly assumed Bruce was now famed director Bruce McFeeney, a well-known, one-time lover of Wynonna's. They attempted to get a statement from his office, or better yet from Bruce himself, but all the papers got were threats of legal action if they took it any further.

(30)

COLD CASE

The LA detectives had not come up with any person of interest in the Wynonna Bertrand murder after constantly going over all the evidence and interviewing those involved numerous times. No clues at all had been found except the knife, which only revealed it was one from the aircraft. That is all they had come up with so far. Ian Church was getting pressure from his superiors to find the murderer and close the case and he was beyond frustrated. The hardest part for him to get over was the fact that he must have been talking face-to-face with the murderer without ever knowing it.

Wynonna's funeral was held two weeks after her murder in Los Angeles. The street surrounding the church was packed with people wanting to get a look and take their pictures. Many of Wynonna's fans were in attendance—mainly her usual followers consisting of gay men who saw her as the queen diva and bitch to end all bitches. A few came dressed in drag or as some of her more memorable characters. Also in attendance were a few studio bosses, producers and directors, although most studios just sent a representative. The press noted and reported a lack of high-list celebrities. Wynonna's papers did not reveal a will, so unless a suitable relative came forward to claim her estate—of which about twenty-five had tried and failed, to make the courts believe they were her long lost child—her only beneficiary would be Uncle Sam.

Peter and Orla were brought in for more questioning. They were asked again how and why the bathroom had evidence of being wiped clean, but no cloth or towels were ever found in either the bathroom waste or the garbage that the forensics team removed from the plane. This was a ploy to ask the same question after some time had passed, to see if the person had the same answer.

The question was answered again when Peter explained about the situation with Jonathon. "We did have a situation with a passenger who fell ill and I did supply him with some towels so he could clean up. He probably used them to wipe over the bathroom as well as tidy himself. He took the soiled towels along with his garments in a plastic bag when he left," Peter told them.

Orla did manage to go on her vacation, but only after she gave all the relevant information of her trip to Detective Church. She explained the dealings she had with Wynonna throughout the flight and told them how Wynonna was acting. Once she knew Wynonna was asleep, she didn't attend to her at all for the last few hours of the flight, until she had found her.

Orla had a marvelous time on her trip to Thailand and was now making plans for her next adventure. The death of Wynonna was a turning point in Orla's life. She decided to live life to the fullest and was thinking of finding someone special to spend some time with. She was thinking of Paul Danielson and wondered where he was now.

Peter and James stayed in contact with Craig, who introduced them to Patrick on the night they landed in LA. Along with Rebecca and Paul, they went out to dinner that night and had a great time. Craig had originally thought about meeting them at the *Queen Mary*, but Patrick insisted they come by the new house and they decided to dine at a local restaurant instead. They had yet to work with Stu and Max, but any revenge had been erased after Stu and Max's passionate kiss. They treated them different now that the cat was out of the bag. James even had thoughts of inviting them out to dinner, if and when the chance ever presented itself.

James continued to swim each morning and informed Peter he was thinking of trying out for a coaching position at the local pool.

Peter decided to attend a cooking course; he had been thinking his days as a flight attendant may be coming to a close and he wanted to do something in which he was interested. It seemed Wynonna's death had a similar effect on him as it did with Orla and he decided life was too short to waste.

Craig Lewis wasn't questioned again after the flight. His story, verified by Peter and Orla, made him an innocent man and not a person of interest to the police. He came home to find Patrick had done a fabulous job decorating their new Malibu home. He called Jacob as soon as he could to tell him about Wynonna. Jacob had already heard, which confused Craig because he made the call as soon as he got into the limo. Nobody could keep anything from Jacob. Once Craig was back at work, he told Jacob about the New York locations and about a new person in whom he might be interested. Jacob wanted to know more, but Craig could only describe Paul to him the best he could and they would have to wait to see if Paul called. Craig had Paul's contact number but didn't give it to Jacob just yet. He was sure Paul was going to call because both James and Peter told him the night they went to dinner that he would be a natural in front of a camera.

There was another celebration in Craig's life. Patrick had just received the contract to completely decorate George Clooney's recently purchased mansion in the Hollywood hills. It would bring in big bucks and Patrick told him once it was done, they would fly to Europe for a first-class vacation.

Since their impromptu announcement made on board, Adam and Charlotte had been inseparable. Neither gave the embarrassing situation another thought and now they were happy in one another's company. They applied to work together on as many shifts as possible and Adam asked Charlotte to move in with him. They had yet to join the mile-high club, but as Charlotte told Rebecca, "I prefer the nine-inch club, if you know what I mean." After a severe dressing down by Captain Havilland, no further action was taken by Trans County Airways over the incident with the PA system.

Rebecca thought Patrick and Craig's new home was the most beautiful place she had ever seen. The day after their dinner with

Peter, James and Paul, she asked Craig and Patrick about her moving nearby. She knew it was time to move out of her parents' home and start her life. Patrick knew of a few rental properties a few blocks away, so they went to see them. Rebecca fell for all of them but settled on a two-bedroom apartment in a quiet, tree-lined street opposite a large park. Of course, she asked Patrick if he would help her decorate and while Craig went off to work, they both went shopping. She showed Patrick the type of furniture she liked and when she went off to look at some other smaller items, Patrick paid for all the bits and pieces she had showed him. He would not hear a word about it, only saying that she was to have them over for dinner when she was settled.

Captain Havilland flew the return flight back to JFK that afternoon along with Stu and Max. The only other member of the crew from the previous flight was Bryson. After meeting with the Trans County management concerning the details of Wynonna's death, along with the Adam and Charlotte incident, Billy took an extra two days off to spend more time with his wife; they took a trip to Vermont and relaxed. Wynonna's death was the first major incident on any flight piloted by Captain Havilland. He wanted a clean record, not that Wynonna's death had anything to do with him; it would not show up on any official record. He just wanted his record to be a clean one in his own mind.

Stuart Orwin was sitting for some exams, which would see him become a full-time captain for Trans County Airways. He needed to sit through two more exams and pass the simulator test and it wasn't long before he found out he had passed with top honors. When it was time for the award ceremony, he announced he would take his longtime companion and lover, Max Alexander.

Max was so excited about Stu's promotion; it meant he and Stu could begin to make some real plans together. He even put their grievances concerning Peter and James to rest by asking them to dinner. Both couples became quite close and now spent a great deal of time together.

Max never did like lying to his colleagues, but he thought if the airline knew about the two of them, then the chances of Stu making captain might be hurt. As it turned out, Max had no reason to worry because the Trans County management made them front-page news on the monthly newsletter.

Grace went back to her normal position of head flight attendant. She actually crewed the return flight that the Greats traveled on back to New York. She asked them how they enjoyed their trip and was regaled with lots of stories. She never did find out whether they were club members, although she believed they were. Upon her return, she told Kane all about them. He seemed a bit too interested for her liking.

When Bryson returned to New York, he had a message that his wife had been taken to the hospital because of complications with her pregnancy. He arrived to find she had been suffering phantom pains, which scared the daylights out of him. He asked if he could be placed on short-haul flights until the baby was born. Trans County Airways did better than that by giving him paid leave. Four days later, he was a proud father of a beautiful baby girl, whom they named Danielle. Mother and baby were both doing well. Father Bryson was over the moon and still sang Barry White songs.

Gavin and Douglas had a great time in New York, telling all their friends about the clubs. Gavin was most excited about Splash; he told his friends that the club was decorated like one big bathroom. There were showers behind the bar where guys danced wearing Speedos and all the walls were tiled. He thought New York was the greatest place he had ever seen. Doug told them about the guy he picked up one night who asked him to dance in the middle of Times Square—and they did, all the way to his apartment.

Norman and Katherine Great had the trip of a lifetime—literally, because so far it had been their only trip. They could not stop talking about Disneyland and Hollywood. They even saw Kirstie Alley in a store. One thing they decided to leave out was their own version of in-flight entertainment; they didn't think their family and friends would approve. Their newfound club friends did approve, though and they continued to remain in contact with each other.

Owen and Anna didn't have any more rallies planned, so they settled back in their Long Beach apartment—not that it was a bad thing, because they had some company. Norman and Katherine paid them a visit and spent a life-changing experience with them—or rather, wife-changing!

Jennifer Stone had taken a few days off after the fight to LA. The death on board shook her up, so she decided to stay in LA to calm her nerves. She was resting by the hotel pool when a hotel waiter asked her if she desired anything. Jen did not believe in love at first sight, but this was as close as it got. Jack was a sometime waiter at the Renaissance Hotel at LAX; the remainder of his time was devoted to his writing. He had had a book published with small success and was finishing up his second book. Jen and Jack became as close as two people could get in just two days, but they decided to keep in touch. Jen was due for some time off, so she told Jack she would call him with the dates and they could get together and see where their relationship was headed. As it turned out, after a year of dating, they headed straight toward the altar.

Millie and Thelma had the time of their lives in LA. They were a hit at the hotel, especially at breakfast time. Both women loved the idea of the "all you can eat" buffet and they regularly made two and sometimes three trips. The hotel staff was in tears most of the time and the hotel management decided to give them a free dinner on their last night. They also got use of the hotel limo to take them wherever they wanted to go.

"You see those pancakes they have? I got to get me some more of those. Gonna get me some of that bacon and sausage as well," Thelma said.

Millie replied, "Get some of those donuts, the jelly kind. We can stash them for later. Girl, I haven't eaten this good in a long time. You think they got Pop Tarts?"

Thelma was the day planner on this trip. She always started with, "Let's get downstairs before they finish breakfast." While they were at breakfast, she would go through the day's itinerary, basically discussing where lunch should be. At lunch the conversation turned to where dinner should be. Wherever else they ended up would just be to fill in time until the next meal. They loved it.

Paul Danielson eventually made a call to Craig Lewis a few days after their dinner. He told him he was ready to give the acting thing a try and had some spare time. He thought, *Why not see if I have what it takes?* Craig was beside himself with excitement because he knew Paul did have what it takes. He set up an interview with Jacob for the following day and told Paul to dress casual and be himself. Craig said Jacob always held his meetings at a local restaurant around lunchtime and he gave Paul the address and time. Craig was already there when Paul arrived. Jacob was running about fifteen minutes late, which gave Craig the opportunity to chat with Paul and give him some more pointers. Paul did not say much and seemed a bit nervous. Craig told him not to worry and to relax, adding that this was not a screen test, just a chance to for Jacob to meet him.

Jacob arrived and was introduced to Paul. He immediately said Paul was perfect for a character he had in mind for his next project. He told him he would need him to do a screen test to see if his looks transferred to film and he would need to do a read-through. "Are you available this afternoon? I can have something set up in about two hours if you're interested," Jacob said.

All Paul's nervousness disappeared and he actually seemed excited by it all. "I haven't got anything planned for the time I'm here—just touristy stuff. So why not? I'll give it a go. I have an idea I've been working on for a play. My friend in New York is an actor and I was playing around writing some stuff for him. Do you want to hear it?" Paul said.

"Not at this moment, because I'm running late and need to set up your screen test. Run it by Craig and he can fill me in," Jacob told him.

After Jacob left, Craig asked Paul how he felt about Jacob and Paul said he was actually getting into the whole movie idea. He said he would do his best at the screen test and whatever happened, happened.

Craig told him he would be there with him for support and he would try to get the lines Paul would need to run through so he could practice. Craig already knew the part Jacob wanted Paul for and if the guy didn't freeze up, he should ace it.

James Austin

"Now tell me about this play," Craig prompted.

"Well, basically it's about a boy who grew up knowing he was adopted. Eventually, after a few years, he finds his birth mother only to find she wants nothing to do with him. Feeling rejected and hurt, he sets out to hurt her like she hurt him. He soon finds out she is booked on a flight to LA and decides to follow her and carry out her murder there, away from where he lives. He books himself on the same flight so as not to lose track of her. Luck is on his side when he gets his chance to kill her while on board a flight from New York to Los Angeles . . ."